James Beard has spent most of his working life in education; teaching and lecturing at every level, after early experience in market research. He took up writing in retirement 'to escape boredom' and has submitted two plays in competition, one a piece of musical theatre. He focuses on historical fiction, embracing his own, or family experience and interests. Travel, gardening and community activities are his focus when not on 'grand parenting' duties.

To Mike and Alison
And thank you for
being such good friends

Jim

To Paul, who was larger than life, and who taught us so much of the Dutch way of life.

For my darling wife, and our two grandchildren who 'live' my story, Freya and Elinor.

I am indebted to Maarten Frankenhuis's account of those hidden in Artis Zoo in Amsterdam during WW2 'Overleven in de dierentuin' (and his penguin joke in an interview given to The Republic of Amsterdam Radio). Also to my early readers, and to Artis zoo and Kim who gave me approvals to reference the actual people and events of the time, and to Iris, and to Anton Kras at the Joods Cultureel Kwatier who helped with contemporary photographs, even though— alas—we did not include them in the end.

James Beard

THE WHY QUESTION

AUSTIN MACAULEY PUBLISHERS™

LONDON • CAMBRIDGE • NEW YORK • SHARJAH

A CIP catalogue record for this title is available from the British Library.

ISBN 9781398462120 (Paperback)
ISBN 9781398462762 (ePub e-book)

www.austinmacauley.com

First Published 2023
Austin Macauley Publishers Ltd®
1 Canada Square
Canary Wharf
London
E14 5AA

Almost all the historical events in the story which follows are true. But the story is mine alone, except that each and every person here, though invented, is real to the writer, in character and personality.

I would like to thank Simon West for the cover design.

Remember, Life is for Living

Life's full of beauty and wonderful things
Don't hide in a cage, but instead spread your wings
Remember, life is for living.
Keep your head high, stick your nose in the air.
What others are thinking, why would you care?
Keep your heart warm, the love it will beam
Wherever you go, you shall be queen.
This gift to yourself keeps on giving
Remember, life's for the living.
(Adapted from Dirk Witte, 1885–1932)

Part One

Chapter 1

I will never forget that day we first met. Eleonore and I. She is the new girl in the class. Every other face is familiar from kindergarten and so we are all curious. Who is she and where is she from? But I am stuck on only one thing, so stuck that I fail to notice even the words she is saying.

It's her eyes. They are blue, but not like the misty blue of my classmates, which is the colour of the sea at Den Haag, but a deep and inky blue, like magical pools, forever dissolving and resurrecting themselves. "I'm sorry, I'm staring," I say, but she simply takes me by the hand and leads me to the little line of benches surrounding our work tables beneath the large windows through which you can see the large Montessori Lyceum sign.

"It is not a problem," she says.

So you can imagine the chill, like ice running through my blood, when no more than one year later, Papa says, "I think it's better if you don't spend so much time with Eleonore now." There's no doubting it. Papa has changed. Not, to be honest, completely changed. But little by little, without my really noticing, he is becoming the father I've not known before. As a little girl he would always tell me, "If you always ask the question 'why', you will discover the secrets of the universe." Nowadays I think he is irritated by my 'whys' as if he has to search amongst his mind for a whole list of answers; at other times, he is simply silent. Mama sticks up for him and says I have to understand that things are difficult these days, or that a man doesn't always find these things easy. I don't know much about men, but I am beginning to wonder if he never knew all of the answers anyway. So I decided it is better to stay quiet about my best friend ever. For the time being anyway.

And anyway; there is the little matter of the mystery of the Artis zoo for us to solve.

February 1940, by Eleonore

I am writing something in my workbook because Papi thinks it will help me with my Dutch. Many words here are the same as back home, but they sound completely different to me. "Like a barrel of baboons," says Mamie. Sorry to my new friend Freyja, who I just met at school. We have a pact. She helps me with my Dutch, and I help her with her writing, which is nowhere near as neat and tidy as we Germans do. She always wants to help everyone, and she says that she believes in the goodness of people.

Our school is special. We are all mixed together, older and younger, girls and boys: as Papi says, "Not peas in a pod, more like a basket of fallen apples." I like this idea; it is just the same as the human family. Mamie warns me not always to think too deeply. When I tell Freyja, she says if I don't give up soon, my brain will freeze, just like the canals in wintertime. This has taken me a whole hour, so I will stop for now.

I have to copy out my sentences over and over again to improve my writing. Mama says, "A tidy hand is a tidy mind," which is like lots of things that grown-ups say, which don't make a great deal of sense. Of course, I would much rather be outside, playing with the bricks, planks and sand which completely surround our house. Except when it's 'raining pipe stems', which Eleonore finds very amusing, like lots of things we say here.

Everything about here is quite new or quite unfinished, but yesterday a big yellow crane came and dug a huge triangle patch which they planted with trees, like a miniature forest. Papa tells me that this is an important part of a new Holland, where everyone will have a good place to live and work.

I so much want Eleonore to come here to visit because she is my very special friend. At school, they tell us that we are all part of God's creation and we should be friends with everyone, but perhaps they don't know so much about our feelings? It's not only Eleonore's eyes that seem to stay with me all the time, but also the sound of her voice and the funny way she says things. "So yes, you are quite right, Eleonore." or "It is so true." Mama has explained that every language in the world has a different pattern. I can't tell which, but hers is quite different from the sing-song of Danielle who came here from France. Never mind. We are lucky that where we live is quite near to places that people from all over Holland come to visit – to see Van Gogh's new pictures in the Stedelijk Museum and also our most famous painter ever, whose name I don't always remember. I had to ask Mama for help with the museum spelling and didn't want her to think that I was so stupid that I didn't know our best painter ever. I think we shall soon have our own tram stop too, so it will be easier for

Eleonore. And we may be able to visit the zoo. She says she loves animals.

March 1940

I have got to know my friend really well, so we spend all our time together. Her favourite thing to eat in the whole world is oliebollen, which are like little sweet balls, fried in oil, and she has even taught me how to eat a herring "like a Dutchman", her papa's expression. You hold it by its tail, throw your head back and swallow it whole, like a pelican swallowing a fish. We agree that some grown-up expressions are crazy. We are not Dutchmen, after all.

My spelling is getting better, but Mamie says I have to let her correct my diary in case anyone gets to read it. Freyja still finds it hard to write neatly, but I think it is her brain, which like her writing, never stays still. Her papa is annoying because after she told him about me, he said, "We Dutch are very much like the Germans," and then, much later on, "What is it with these damn Germans?" Both things can't be right, can they? But he has invited me to visit their house, so I am forgiving him.

Freyja and I have been asked to give a joint presentation to the class. The teacher says this is a very Montessori idea, for it's better to do things together rather than on your own. "What were the very first things you noticed when you first came to Holland?" Freyja asks, and that gives us an idea for our project. But we won't mention that the very first thing was the stench of cow…(Mamie has crossed this out), but then she said Holland has more cows than anywhere in the world, and why wouldn't you, if you adored milk and cheese?

Me: What is black and white and red all over, Eleonore?

What is black and white and red all over? I don't know.

Then just guess, Eleonore. Just guess.

What if I can't?

Then say I don't know. What is black and white and red all over? Try again.

You're annoying, Freyja.

Me: A newspaper, silly. It's obvious.

So, you're far better than me at puzzles.

Spell Scheveningen, Eleonore. Can you say it?

Ssche…

No German in the whole world can say it. Always remember that. Okay, once more. Scheveningen.

Spell it.

You're making fun of me. If I can't even say it, how can I spell it?

Spell it. Spell it. Spell it, Eleonore.

Scheven…I give up.

i.t. idiot.

What? I don't get it!

My parents think it will be nice if I bring Eleonore home. One thing we have in common is that we do not have any brothers or sisters. Though Eleonore is never alone, she says, because "How can you be? When Mamie and Papi talk and talk and talk and always have the radio on," and of course, I have lots of friends inside my head. She tells me she has cousins here in Amsterdam, but mostly her family is back in Germany. Her papa is something called a travelling salesman, but I don't know what he sells, except they have a special homecoming every Friday, so it can't be that night. It is just a matter of planning, which I'm good at, except Eleonore says, "No, you're just bossy."

Even though I adore her eyes, that doesn't mean we agree on every single thing. Why should we? Clothes, for example. "Who puts out your clothes in the morning?" I ask.

Eleonore says, "I choose my own, of course. Who else?" That makes me wonder what kind of parents she has. There are vivid colours, and frills and ruffles on everything, but I don't know her well enough to tell her that the colours don't always match and they definitely don't go with her eyes, but I truly wouldn't want to hurt her. Mama says, "We all have minds of our own," but that's an example of that grown-up code, which Eleonore says we have to crack. After all, how can we have other people's minds? There is an English detective called Sherlock Holmes, who is famous here and who can untangle any puzzle put in front of him, including murder. Perhaps we should put him on the case?

April 1940

Things at school are getting a little worrying. Our teacher, Miss Kelter, truly believes in peace amongst all people, but now she is talking to us about war. Yesterday, we all had to pretend to hide underneath our work tables, and some of the little ones cried, so I asked the teacher if I could go to the puppet box to rescue the scruffy little character who helps Saint Nicholas to deliver the Christmas presents. "Look, It's Black Pete and he's squashed underneath all his friends. Who will come and rescue him? He's hidden beneath all the others and must be saved. Otherwise, there will be no presents next year." Everyone tells me that I have a good imagination, unlike the way I say things in Dutch, which is still not good.

"It's only a precaution," says Miss Kelter after we emerge, but I know that times are uncertain. Even though we argue, Freyja and I, how is it possible to hate someone so much that you want to steal their country and even worse? I try not to think about it too much because whatever's happening, it must be far away. And some say it's none of our business anyway. We're only visitors.

We are allowed one telephone call a week.

"Next Saturday then? Will that be okay, Eleonore? And then you could sleep here overnight."

Are you sure they wouldn't mind? Freyja?

(I look at myself in the long mirror facing the phone stand. I look back.)

They really want you to come. And I've told them so much about you.

All the best things?

All the nice things, silly. And Papa says we can put you in a taxi home. You wouldn't want to stay for Sunday anyway.

What's wrong with Sunday? It's not a school day.

Well, there's a draughty old church where all they talk about is the suffering of Christ. And we all have to go. There are a few nice boys, though. (My cheeks in the mirror are blushing.)

We don't go to Church. It sounds awful. What should I wear?

Anything nice, Eleonore. It doesn't matter. But don't forget your night things. I have to tell you one secret, though.

What is it?

You promise not to tell?

(My reflection says, should I really?)

My parents are far too stuffy for their own good.

Too stuffy for their own good?

(I make a pose to show that I'm not stuffy)

Perhaps we need the help of the English detective, Eleonore?

Detective?

He solves mysteries, Eleonore. We should find a clue to help us understand grown-ups.

All the grown-ups in the whole world? That's impossible. We could find murderers, though.

That's what Detective Holmes does. Find murderers.

How do you know?

I saw it in the movies.

Papi says Hitler's a murderer, Freyja.

Hitler? But he's a German like you, isn't he?

Chapter 2

Today is a special day. No, we are not going to the zoo, which I would really like, but the next best thing. We are going to a museum to look at the new sunflower paintings of Van Gogh. The teacher puts up a large screen in the corner of the classroom, and we squat on the floor as she projects glass slides of lots and lots of things he painted and sketched. It's funny to think that not many people liked them at first. Not only are there so very many, but you can't imagine how different the flowers are. Neat petals, blurry petals, large stamens, small stamens, drooping stalks, upright stalks; everything different but you can tell the colours he liked, which are often a kind of yellow; bright yellow, muddy brown, streaky orange. We have a class vote to see which is the favourite flower. "What's yours?" I whisper to Eleonore.

But she only answers, "It's my secret." That takes me by surprise, but then I realise we must all be allowed to have minds of our own.

After our lunch, we take a tram to Vondelpark and have a play about before we walk to the Stedelijk Museum, which is the name written in large letters on our sketchpads. Miss Kelter forms us into pairs in a crocodile line. This is my chance. I don't want to annoy Eleonore, but Dirk, who is one of the boys at church, is a little sweet on me and like all boys, a little bit shy, so I take his hand before he can say "No." He doesn't rush about pretending to drive tanks and fire guns like the others in the class but is thoughtful like Eleonore. We talk every bit of the way and it is amazing how quickly the time goes when you talk. He knows everything about animals and insects.

"What's your favourite?" I ask.

He says, "The wolf." So I promise myself I will take out our encyclopaedia at home and discover more. I like the way his big round spectacles creep along his nose so he looks like the mad professor in the Struwwelpeter books.

Once inside the Museum, which seems like a giant's version of our school and smells a little damp and musty like our canals, we look at the paintings. A lot of them are dark and drab and have lots of old-fashioned people in them, so I am pleased when we arrive at the Van Gogh section. There are squashy banquettes and tables set around and it's here where we will copy one picture onto our pads. I am really dreading this moment because I just can't draw and soon, I see Eleonore is way ahead of me. It's all the twists and turns of colour and shape that confuse me and I want to give up, but then she folds over her pad, hands it to me and takes mine. Miss Kelter is nowhere to be seen. I look over her shoulder as my sunflower takes better shape and almost comes to life. And when it is finished, she very carefully writes beneath, "Drawn by Freyja Scholte." In my exact writing. So miracles do happen.

May 1940

I went to Freyja's house at last. It was a long taxi ride because there are big blocks of concrete and wire across many streets. Lots of our neighbours are newcomers from other places, mostly not even in Holland. Mamie says they come here for many reasons, but mainly because they are not made to feel welcome in their countries. I think we are here for Papi's work because he says, "Business is always better with the Dutch," but I can't really be certain. And I know that they don't want me to worry so much.

My Dutch words are getting better, but I still find it hard to pronounce them. And Freyja and I are finding it hard being Sherlock Holmes. There are so many hundreds of sayings in this language that it's like "opening envelopes with thick wooden gloves." Another grown-up thing to say.

Freyja's house is quite big and airy, and we mainly play outside, until we all walk to an amazing ice-cream place, and I choose a Knickerbocker glory, which she says "is far too greedy" and she will stick to a 'double scoop'. Mine has layers of everything under the sun; thick cream, sparkles, chocolate, vanilla sauce, and so on. She dips into mine with her wooden spoon, licks her lips and says 'Leuk' which is a word sounding like Lekker and which Dutch children say all the time, so I say 'Leuk' too and I feel all melty inside like the ice cream in my glass. Everyone is very quiet at the dining table, which I am not used to, but her papi asked me lots of questions about Germany and that he works in an office doing "lots of important work" with paper. Freyja glances across at me – another mystery. He eats very slowly and chews things so carefully that I almost laugh out loud because it reminds me of a rabbit nibbling its food. And the meal goes on forever and ever. But I'm excited because we have agreed that later on, she will show me how to do ringlets in my hair. When I hold hers in its long strands, it is curlier than mine and it won't keep still and keeps bouncing back which makes us both giggle.

"What are you two up to?" says her mamie, but it is our secret and you don't have to tell grown-ups everything. I really like our fun before bedtime, and I have brought my favourite cloth doll to show, which even though I am quite grown up, I have had and forever, which has straw-coloured plaited hair to help us sleep just in case, but then at the top of the long steep staircase, her mamie places her hand gently on my hand and turns me in one direction as Freyja goes in the other. At least there's a little green sink and washstand in my room, but it just isn't the same.

As her papi put me in the taxi, the next day and gave the man my address, I think I heard something like "So the Jews have crossed the Amstel." Hmm, no idea.

Me: How many minutes, Eleonore?

Quiet. Just concentrate.

But you have the watch. So, okay. What can you see?

"The Montessori way," Freyja. Remember. We're looking, not seeing. Miss Jurgen says If you know what you are seeing, you have already decided what you want to see.

"Just let it wash over you," she says. How crazy is that?

At least we should try. You start, Freyja.

Me: Jumbles of leaves and branches and…

A caterpillar clinging to a leaf.

Look, Eleonore. A black and white bird with a worm.

"That's very good looking, Freyja," as Miss Jurgen would say.

Can you get me a watch, Eleonore?

I'll speak to Papi if you stop nattering.

The grass is tickling my back.

"Feelings, my girls. Feelings." (In the teacher's voice)

Can you look at your watch now, Eleonore?

Two and a half minutes.

Is that long enough?

I'll ask him about the watch.

Papa is not so sure about the Germans anymore. Because we have always been a peaceful country, we won't fight wars but that wouldn't stop the English from coming over here to attack their enemy, would it? I am pleased with myself because I am using the 'why' question whenever I can right now. "The English can be very bloodthirsty," he says, "and they stole big parts of Africa that once belonged to the Dutch." The Germans and the English have always had wars against each other, even though their kings and queens and princes and princesses are all related to each other. Perhaps Eleonore and I are lucky not to have brothers and sisters, otherwise, they might all end up marrying each other and then, who knows?

Our most favourite family trip so far has been the one to Den Haag, which is where our Queen lives. It is quite like a fairytale palace, but the part which she lives in is more like a grand family house. What is amazing is that she became Queen at ten years of age, which is hard to believe, because how could I have ruled the whole of this country only one year ago? My writing is so terrible that no one would be able to read my instructions.

Afterwards, we went up to the top of a building, which looked just like a lighthouse inside with kaleidoscope pictures all around that really was like being on the beach, or in a forest, and every different place you could imagine in real life. You didn't have to close your eyes; you really are there. Also, it looked like it was all painted by a Grand Master. I asked Eleonore why all the paintings I have seen so far are by men, and she said who would do the housework and cooking if things were different? She tells me that this is something called irony, which is what grown-ups do as well as talk in code.

Later, when I had my telephone chat with her, we talked about what Papa had said about wars. She said she couldn't understand why anyone would want to attack the Jews, but that her Mamie had said, "Show me a German, and he will tell you at least a thousand things to hate about Jews." I don't think we know any Jews; in fact, I don't even know what Jewish is. Anyway, to change the subject I read her my nonsense poem for the week. Miss Kelter had read us some nonsense rhymes which she said had been invented by another Englishman who was called Edward Lear. I asked her if he had ever met the man who wrote Sherlock Holmes stories. She said that she did not know, which is a relief as it is not only father who sometimes has problems answering questions.

There was an old woman from Tilburg
Who married this man down in Limburg
She fell into a stream
No one heard her loud scream
And now she's a chunk in an iceberg

I didn't tell Eleonore that I had help with this one. A lot of help.

June 1940

So many things have happened since I last wrote, so it is a complete jumble in my head. First, we weren't allowed to go to school because we are safer at home. I tried to telephone Freyja because I was missing her, and I knew that she could explain a few things, but all I heard was buzzing and clicking and no one replied. Papi tells me that there are lots of Germans here now, so I can't see why he shouldn't be pleased, but what is the point of trying to learn Dutch properly if we'll all end up speaking German? He also tells me the Dutch Queen has gone to England to live, and we all sat around the radio to hear her speak. Mamie says she is our Queen now and I like that idea. She has a lovely firm voice and though I didn't understand everything, I caught the word 'vrijheid' – freedom – which I do know, and also much about evildoers. When I was little, my favourite aunty would read me and my cousins' lots of stories, and one was about wicked Frederick, who tormented humans and animals. I can't remember the ending, but in most stories, the good characters win and the evildoers die, so things shouldn't be so bad. But I worry most at bedtime because the Germans have switched off all the streetlights, and there's no longer a finger of magic dust showing through the curtains. I won't write any more now because, alongside all the jumble in my head, I know there is something wrong. And Freyja tells me the zoo is closed for now. Why would anyone want to do that? Unless they think the Germans might bomb it like they did in Rotterdam.

Chapter 3

Papa says if you can't telephone Eleonore, because she must be really worried about me, why not take my nonsense poem to school? We have agreed that they have to be about water because we have so much of it here in Holland.

There was an old fella from Breda
Who went to sea in a freighter
There was so great a swell
That he slipped and he fell
And now in the ocean does dwell

She said that hers was funnier than mine, so I told her that her parents are better at writing nonsense poems, and now we both know "the monkey is out of the sleeve". She finds that saying hilarious. For now, we will put nonsense rhymes to bed and concentrate on our class presentation instead. She has written a list of everything that was new and surprising when she first came to our country, and so far we have oliebollen, of course, bicycles of every shape and size, canals, windmills, clogs, wonky houses, the sound of trams; the list goes on. She was surprised to discover there is mostly not a single hill or mountain here, but there is a brand new sound for everyone now, which is heavy marching boots, which ring just like iron on an anvil. Mama has told me to keep well away from the boots. My uncle and aunt, Paul and Myrese came to our house to listen to the Queen's speech, and afterwards, all the grownups argued, because "did she really want to go to England?" or was it "just too dangerous for the navy boat to take her all the way to America?" It seems grown-ups not only speak in riddles, but they can't really agree about things lots of the time. So how can children know where they stand about the Germans? At least Eleonore will be able to talk to them and ask for herself.

June 1940

Something very wonderful has happened here, even if things are turning out very bad. Because we don't like the Germans being around, we have to show them something that will teach them a lesson. You have to know that the Queen's daughter fell in love with a German man (he's a prince) but to show he loves the Dutch people, he always wears a flower on his jacket on the Queen's birthday. So in this horrible year, everybody in Holland has been asked to sport the same white carnation in their buttonholes, or wherever they liked. We took a walk with my cousins Erin and Reuben and surprise; every window is filled with bunches of white flowers, in plant pots, and jam jars, and any old thing. I would like to have a flower shop when I grow up and if we can just get rid of these rotten Nazis, as Papi calls them, we will carry on with this tradition. That should make me very rich indeed. I didn't tell you that Erin and Reuben came to Holland with Aunty Gabbi and Uncle Jurgen before we arrived to 'pave the way'; another strange expression. So that's how I got to have cousins, of course.

Me: "Dames en Heren. I would like to introduce my dear friend Eleonore to you. She is a guest in my country and I would like you all to be kind to her. Just remember how you would feel if you were in a really dark place, and you didn't recognise a single thing around you. Eleonore? Your turn."

We are in a tall van with windows all around. I can see long rivers with flat dark boats, but the water is not curvy but runs absolutely straight. It seems hours since we said goodbye to our friends. Although I try to be brave, I can see Mamie has been crying. I cried too when we had to leave our pets behind.

Do you remember your first day at school and you saw your mother walk away? Imagine.

At first; many children are just like me on their bicycles, but riding altogether, hands on shoulders, or stretched out to hold the other. And giant windmills wherever you looked. I hear the swoosh as the wind blows through their sails, and the cows mooing in the fields. Sometimes they stand stock-still. Do they know something we don't know? The grass is so green, but you can hardly see a blade for the spread of animals. Are we there yet, Mamie?

Me: Have you ever been lost, and worry that you will never get back home?

We are stopped by a food van at the side of the road. There is a flag waving on the roof with stripes of red, white and blue going sideways, and Papi tells me that this is the flag of the Dutch Republic and we should always respect it, for they took us in. I nibble at a little golden ball dripping with sugar. The very first taste of my new country.

Imagine. Our guest has only ever seen flags of red and black, with an ugly symbol that looks like someone kicking and hurting another.

"Freyja?"

"Yes, Miss Kelter?"

"Today, we are thinking of the sights and sounds of Holland."

"But my Uncle…"

"Your Uncle would be most pleased by your welcoming your new friend. So let Eleonore proceed." (This is a word the teacher uses a lot. Nearly every single day.)

I think that little sugary treat is saying "Hello" to me. Now the countryside is getting more and more like home. But not a hill in sight. The ground is sandy, the trees like Christmas. I see brightly coloured train carriages following a puffing billy, and it starts to get dark. "When are we going to get there?" I ask.

Me: Eleonore has arrived in the winter, the coldest time of the year.

The moon reflects on an icy canal, and we drive through little villages where no one closes their curtains so that you can see everything that is happening inside. People cooking, tidying, listening to the radio. I even see two people arm in arm dancing.

I tell her that we Dutch do not draw our curtains because we have nothing to hide.

I thank her, but my secret is that it is the very first Dutch saying I do not understand. I really will have to learn to speak and think and write like a Dutch person, and then perhaps all will be revealed.

Has anything changed since the Germans arrived? Of course, you see their soldiers on the street, but they always have Dutch policemen with them, so that's alright. And Papa says they are always polite. Eleonore says it might be more difficult to visit her house, and I must admit that makes me sad. At the moment, she doesn't really know why, but I know she will tell me when she does. But Mama has promised that she will take me and Eleonore and her cousins to the Amsterdam Zoo – called Artis – when it opens once more because it is in their neighbourhood. Mama says, "The new man at the zoo was at school with me, and he is very 'high up', so he will give us a special personal tour." The zoo is very old, and its first animals were part of a travelling circus. Can you imagine it? A grisly grey elephant with a long wavy trunk leading a procession of lions, tigers, hyenas, polar bears, kangaroos, wildebeests right through the streets of Amsterdam. Everyone watching and waving, and the noise and hubbub! There was even a snake, which was eight times as long as I am tall, or so Mama tells me. And the best Dutch art is not only in the Rijksmuseum, but a lot is also shown at the zoo, where there is some famous modern sculptors' work. Eleonore tells me on the telephone, which seems to be working again, that some of her friends go there on Fridays to buy the Saturday tickets, but why not go straight there on Saturdays? Another puzzle for the English detective. The only thing that I worry about is how would she feel if I asked Mama to invite Dirk to the trip as well.

Chapter 4

July 1940

We are going to have to try to be much more grown-up now that we might be in danger, so I am going to call mummy 'Mother' instead. Freyja says the Dutch expression for staying strong is 'to have hair on one's teeth' and I am going to ask Freyja whether it's time to call her mummy, Moeder, which is the Dutch word for Mother. Maybe it's best if we both do the same thing and use 'Moeder'; otherwise, it gets very confusing? And why do words have to keep changing anyway?

I am so excited about going to Artis. We Germans love zoos as much as anybody. Many centuries ago, when the Romans conquered Germany and Holland and lots of other places in the world, they gave their own names to everything they discovered, including plants and animals. I haven't told Freyja that Papi had begun to teach me the Roman names for things, which he says will be of great help when I become a physician or a lawyer one day. So when we were sketching the sunflowers in the museum and Freyja talked about wobbly stalks, for instance, I could picture another word in my head – pendunculus – which strictly means foot, the foot of the plant. There are lots of other plant words like this too and Papi says I will find them easy to learn because not only am I learning Dutch, but the teachers have also started to teach us some simple words of English. But then why did he say, "Soon enough the Germans will stop you from learning English," and so things are as muddled as ever. What is that all about? And perhaps I should talk to Freyja about calling our papi's "Father" if we are going to say, Moeder? Mamie's right. I do think too much.

The Wolf – Canis lupus. The most dog-like species in almost every part of the world. Dirk cuts carefully around the belly and legs of his new picture, a rare African golden wolf. His pad is filled with wolves of all different shapes and sizes, and coyotes and jackals, which are relatives. But what they have in common is their large and heavy heads, large teeth, and small and triangular ears. For warmth, the wolf has a dense and fluffy coat. He sticks his pictures onto large outline prints of the world and is a little bit disappointed that the wolf population is dying out in most of the places they were once settled. For a long time, he has been sure that he only needs his wolves and his wolf-lists to be the happiest boy in Amsterdam, but now that he has met Freyja, he is having a rethink. Girls are different from wolves, of course, but he knows that wolves are very faithful and stay together in packs. When they held hands on the way to the museum, it felt just like he had joined his mate in the pack, but it also made him feel wobbly inside. To be honest, he envies wolves for their brilliant eyesight, which is as good as humans, unlike his own, which has been poor for as long as he can remember, and he wonders if Freyja would like him more if he didn't wear spectacles. If they grow up and have children together, he knows that she would be a good mother, just like the wolf who gave its milk to the two starving twins who founded the Roman Empire, Romulus and Remus.

I wonder if it's normal? I mean, I probably think about Eleonore more than any other person on the planet and the worst thing, which I shouldn't tell, is probably sometimes more than Moeder. If I kept a diary like Eleonore, I couldn't even write that. I wonder if I should ask about it, and I am trying to get enough courage for when I can get Uncle Paul and Aunt Myrese alone, who I know would help, but that might not be for a very long time. The last time they visited I had to cry myself to sleep because they and my parents had a very angry shouting match about what I do not know, but of course, it had to be mainly about the Germans, whom Paul calls the Nazis. I can't say I really know the difference, but one is bad and the other not so. That is clear. Anyway, the next day in school, when we were on outdoor play, I asked Eleonore. I don't mean the way I think about her – that will have to wait until a grown-up can help, but the other German thing.

"They were all born German, Freyja, just like me, but something happened to them."

"But you said everybody has a good heart, Eleonore."

"Everyone has a good heart, Freyja, but it can be poisoned by the mind, however hard you try.

"The ones that are poisoned are called Nazis."

"That doesn't make much sense at all. Where is the poison? Who has it?"

"The poison is called ideas, Freyja. To make people Nazis, you tell them that they are the best people in the creation and much better than the rest."

"Is that all it takes to be a Nazi? To think you are the best."

"No Freyja. That's not all. You also have to tell them who are the worst people."

"So, who are the worst?"

That look, I know, will never ever leave me. It's that one where Eleonore answers a question with her 'unspoken' answer, one that doesn't need words. At first silence, then a tiny arch of her brow. And it's now I know I adore her for something even greater than those eyes, the colour of the deepest sea. I love her for her wisdom.

Chapter 5

August 1940

This is a long piece of writing because lots and lots happened on that day, and something quite strange, so maybe I need to think about whether I should show this to Moeder. The only disappointing thing is that Freyja brought Dirk along.

It dawned a really hot sunny day, and I was still a little bit sleepy because I had been so excited the previous night, that I could hardly sleep. My cousins, Reuben and Erin, came to stay and that is maybe the other reason, for we spent hours deciding which are our favourite animals and mammals of all time. Erin is the youngest cousin, and all she could talk about was fish, so we make a wish that there is an aquarium there. Reuben is a typical lions and tigers boy, but neither could really understand when I said, "As God made all the creatures, I love them all equally, and I want to learn everything there is to know about them." After our visit, I began to think that perhaps if I didn't become a doctor or a lawyer, I might like to do some work or other in a zoo.

At the gate, we all meet up with Mr Sunier, who is the important friend of Freyja's mother, although I don't know why. He explains a little bit about the zoo, but also that we would see some artwork, which also makes Artis famous around the world. I really like that we all march in through the gate without paying, and everyone is calling us "Young sir", or "Madam".

There was an aquarium!

"Now, which one of you likes fish?" I understand enough about grown-ups to guess that someone had already told Mr Sunier about Erin. So that's where we visit first. We can go right underneath the tank, and even see the largest creatures like baby sharks right around, from their streaky blue tummies to their spear-like snouts. She really doesn't ever want to leave.

"And I also believe one young lady here is very talented at art?"

"That's ever-so-modest Eleonore." rings out a voice, which is learning more about something grown-ups call sarcasm. Freyja, naturally, is always truthful. So that means a visit to a room Mr Sunier calls a studio, right at the top of the zoo.

We all cram into the lift, which wobbles itself up and up, and Reuben isn't sure whether we will ever get out alive. Dirk has been very quiet during our visit so far, and I wonder whether it's because of me. And then I put aside my wondering, for now, we are in an Aladdin's cave of colour, of rags and cloths, of paints and brushes, of discarded paper and a very tall handsome man called Jaap Kaas, who is a famous sculptor. All around the room, which has huge windows open to the sky, are cupboards and shelves and racks, perched on them are; wildebeests, hippopotami, lions, all in perfect miniature, and polished as if within an inch of their lives. Quite magical they are too, with their marble browns and blacks and greys: sleek as greyhounds in some; bulbous or sinuous in others.

I shall have to stop here, for my hand is aching, but I'm sure you can see that my writing in my new language is getting better.

Zoo Day was unforgettable, but Papa wouldn't come in the end. He says, "Freyja, why lock animals up behind bars as if they are criminals?" but he might have been in for a big surprise had he changed his mind. Dirk is joining us too because he wants to see the wolves, which are his passion. I believe that's because his parents won't let him have a dog, which nearly all families have here, and that is the nearest that he can get.

We take the tram towards the part of the city where Eleonore lives. The houses are much older here and there are many people out on the streets. Some look very strange, with their big bushy beards and curls of hair hanging by their ears. I have only seen ringlets on girls before, but these are definitely men, some of whom wear enormous hats. If they were birds, they would be crows; for they are very darkly dressed, there's no vivid colour or finery and they're just a little bit untidy. I hope Eleonore's father doesn't dress like that. But I glimpse the bustling markets, which I would love to visit someday soon, where the stalls display all kinds of bright and vivid materials and clothes, of trinkets, and bobbins, and sparkling jewellery, and everyday things like pegs and brushes.

Once inside the zoo, I can't resist some people spotting. There are lots of German soldiers who I know are German because they look much smarter than our policemen, and anyway, Dirk knows as much about soldiers as wolves; their regimental flashes on their tunics, etc. His favourite joke is to ask "What is that German soldier called?", the answer to which is always 'Wolfgang', which he finds hilarious because there aren't any 'Liongangs' or 'Tigergangs', but I think it just shows a one-track mind, which is one of the things about Dirk I don't think I could live with. But soon ahead, we spot a great assembly of people and shouts and hubbub, which must be something special. You do not need to wonder for long, however, because I can see the attraction at a distance. Enormous mountain peaks surrounded by rocks and bushes and a goat perched at the very top. But where are the cages and bars? Just the time for a why question. The important man who accompanies us and wants to be called Mr Armand tells us cages and bars aren't natural to the animals. He pulls us closer. Yes, that really is water and a wide moat that doesn't so much to keep the animals in as keeping the people out. And climbing amongst the rocks are goats and monkeys and all manner of things. "But no eagles, or bats, or owls, or any flying creatures," says Mr Armand. "That's our next big challenge."

I love Mr Armand immediately with his big walrus moustache and friendliness to children and I wonder once more about calling Papa 'Father' in future because is that a better name for a person who doesn't believe in miraculous ways of making every life happier, even including animals? If only Mr Armand could rule the world.

August 1940

I am writing this down right away after a nap because I can't get it out of my mind. I suppose that's the reason why people write things down in books; to get things out of their minds and to get them into other people.

We set off to the wolves' enclosure, Moeder, Freyja, Reuben, Dirk, Erin, me and Mr Sunier, who now likes us to call him Mr Armand, which is much friendlier. Dirk has brought his father's binoculars for close-up viewing, to spot this and that, and all afternoon has been lagging behind, sweeping the scene for sea-lions, for giraffes, even the smallest of mammals and insects. But what he is really looking forward to most of all is wolves.

We arrive at the enclosure and settle down to watch. It's behind a wide trench and is built as if it were a natural rocky landscape. That means the wolves can roam up and down their hills and drink from their pools uninterrupted. I am fascinated by the twists and turns of the caverns and the natural breaks in the rocks, providing shelter and resting space. But then – my eyes deceive me. Or do they? Just a momentary glimpse, but I am certain that I spotted something quite out of place; something quite unusual within a rocky cranny. And it doesn't belong to the wolf world, or does it?

"Dirk? Can I borrow your binoculars? Just for a moment. I need to check." Being a boy, he just has to give me a long lecture on how to adjust the lens with the focus wheel, but he is helpful enough to help me hold the eye pieces rock steady. I aim for the spot. "What colour are wolf's eyes, Dirk?" I ask.

"Mainly orange," he replies.

"Not green?"

"Very rarely green, especially as these aren't wolf-dogs."

"And do they grow little bristles below their noses?"

Mr Armand seems a little bit agitated at all this, sweeps the binoculars up away from my face and makes a kind of joke remark. "Do they ever put on their spectacles, Dirk, my wolves?" And then, to lighten the moment. "Tell me, anyone. A question, why do German soldiers always visit the penguins first of all? Because they wear little uniforms, and they all march in straight lines."

Chapter 6

A man alone. During daylight hours, he has the freedom to walk. A talented artist, most would say. At night, he lives in fear. Every little move he makes, and the furious scratching on the door. He dreams of being eaten alive. He is hidden next to the bear enclosure.

A woman and her two small children. They cling onto the handholds beneath the large wooden garage doors laid over the zoo moat. They are cold and wet. The water is beneath them.

An old asthmatic. He dwells in the world of zebras and wildebeests. The stables are foul-smelling, and daily are mucked out into the waste corner, which he inhabits at night.

Mr Armand walks with us to the exit. Along the way, he tells us why he loves his zoo. He sounds a little like the preacher in our draughty Church. "It isn't ever about money, dear children; We are all here as scientists and explorers of the natural world, which, never forget, is endangered, and always under attack. Our one and only purpose is to protect the animal kingdom." And then he adds, as an afterthought almost, "Until the end of time." I like that phrase, but I think this is all a little bit deep for Dirk, whose obsession with wolves, I'm still sure, is based mainly on his real craving for a dog. But we don't have a dog either, so that doesn't make complete sense. Dirk hasn't even noticed me once, so I think Moeder is right in what she said about men, that they don't always find things easy. I'm disappointed that now it is time we must say goodbye and didn't have time for the reptile house, which I mention to Mr Armand, who is deep in conversation with Moeder. But right then he says, "Don't worry. I have a surprise for you." And once there, he ushers us to squeeze into the little office by the turnstile and he takes out a bundle of official-looking forms and says, "I'd like to think that you will come to the zoo whenever you can. And then you will see even more. Every one of you. So I shall authorise an entry pass for your visits. I know your dear mother well, of course, Freyja, but our artist friend here, I shall need some details," – taking a pen – "just your name and address, Eleonore. That will suffice." Again, he reminds me of most of our rather proper priests and the grown-up words he uses.

"Grossman, Eleonore," she replies, "I live at 197a Beethovenstraat, Amsterdam." I believe that is the very first time ever I notice she has a surname.

And then he adds, seemingly to Eleonore, "Don't worry about our penguin-lovers, my dear. We can take care of them."

When Moeder gets me and Dirk home, I make a start with another famous English writer; Rudyard Kipling's 'The Jungle Book', which Papa has found for me. It is all about wolves. That should impress Dirk.

August 1940

Scanning the wolf rock mountain, I caught a glint, just a sliver of light which I first thought must be mineral in the rock face. But there is no doubt. Above the lower cave, a circular hole the size of a person's head and a pair of spectacles! At first, I thought I was seeing the reflection of my own pupils in the eyepieces. But these eyes are not of the deepest blue, but green, and that is most clearly a face. And so there is a person in the cave.

Chapter 7

Great news. I have been invited to Eleonore's eleventh birthday party, and I haven't been to her apartment for such a long time. My parents are happy about it, as long as Uncle Paul, who has the grand name of Paul de Groot, goes with me there. With that name, I always imagine him sitting on a throne in a grand palace, but then he is far too much fun to be that important. He is an actor in a theatre troupe, so I suppose he has to have lots of different voices. For a start, he never takes anything seriously, and he makes a joke of every little thing. I have on my warm felt coat with a little fur trim and I'm allowed to take my wallet with the knitted cotton neck strap, as long as I keep it around my shoulders. Papa has been very kind and he has doubled my savings to help buy a special present. So perhaps I'll give some more thought to whether I should stop calling him 'Daddy'. Though many things are getting more difficult to find in the shops. I am clutching, wrapped in shiny red paper, a beautiful cashmere cardigan, which Mama suggested. It is blue wool to match her eyes.

On Saturdays, everywhere is busier than usual. I have a little panic attack on the tram as I get briefly separated from Uncle Paul, but I remember the name of the stop, and the conductor calls out all the next names as soon as the little tinkling sound of each departure has sounded. You have to hold on for dear life as the tram hurtles round the corners of the shops and theatres and over the canal bridges, the wheels squealing out our arrival.

It's only a short walk to the address that Eleonore has written on a cardboard slip, which she calls her 'business card', in writing so neat that it seems as if it has been printed by a machine. There are endless stairs to the fourth floor, but I know we're nearly there because I can hear an explosion of excited voices. I just keep hoping she will notice me amongst all her family and friends.

We crowd around the door, as we have all arrived at the same time, but I am relieved that I don't see any of the 'crows' who were in the street. Above the hubbub, "Eleonore" "Eleonore," over and over, as if she is the centre of the world. Which today, of course, she is. And then we are let in. Or nearly in, because some are reaching to touch the frame of the door as they enter, which slows us down considerably. Another Sherlock Holmes mystery? But one which Uncle Paul, who knows everything about everything he will explain.

It is the best party I have ever been to. The grown-ups disappear into another part of the building, including Uncle Paul, whom Eleonore tells me later becomes her papi's immediate best friend. She is looking so lovely and she's having a 'matching day'; which I tell her when everything goes with everything else. The black beaded long dress which I instantly envy, patent shoes and long white socks, a tortoiseshell Alice band which glints under the lights. But she's surrounded once again and now there's a game of musical chairs to enjoy where you sit down when the music starts, and not stops as is normal. There's also a blindfold game where you get to spin around and around until you're almost dizzy, and then you choose a person from the circle. You give a kiss and if it's the same sex, you're out. This took a long time because some boys made the most of it, but secretly I would much rather be kissing Eleonore. And then, after the games; "Who wants to go to the market?" her moeder asks.

"Yes, please," for I've heard it's much better than the one at Waterlooplein; much much more for children, with its candy floss, ice cream, roasting nuts, hurdy-gurdy man, and a cripple with a white stick and a monkey whom everyone pays special respect to, as he was wounded fighting for the Belgians in the First World War. He has a sign which says just that.

Eleonore takes me aside and walks me to a stall – just we two – and together we buy two-eternity bands. "Give me your wrist, Freyja," she says and gently places hers there, and I do the same for her. I'm secretly pleased that Dirk is not around.

Back indoors, the other adults join us. Her mother tells how wonderfully kind and thoughtful Eleonore is, which of course, we all know anyway. And now we are each handed a piece of fruit, which is brilliantly speckled red and yellow. "It's from the East and is called pitaya and it looks just like a dragon." When we are seated, and before we can eat, Moeder says and others join in, "Blessed are you, Lord God, King of the Universe, who has granted us life, sustained us and has helped us reach this very special occasion." And as we leave later with Uncle Paul a little unsteady on his feet, I feel behind the open door to reach to its frame. Screwed there is a tiny metal case. I have an overwhelming desire to touch it.

September 1940

"Now it's my turn to give you a present," I say to Freyja, after our class on Dutch culture. I have been dying to hand it over, but I have had to wait patiently, through Rembrandt, who we learn is the world's best painter, Spinoza, who invented a new way of thinking, and Petrus Cuypers, the builder who built the Rijksmuseum and the Railway Station. Because I already paint a little, I know that Rembrandt didn't do many flowers, so there's nothing much of his for me to admire or copy, but how can anyone invent thinking?

The lesson went on, even though I probably know more about Holland than Germany now, but something really is "burning a hole in my pocket." Can you see? I am learning to say things in the Dutch way.

Finally. "Close your eyes, Freyja. Tight and now. Think what it could be?"

"How am I expected...?"

"Then just guess."

There is no way she will guess right because with Freyja, some things stick and some things don't and it doesn't really bother me because they are the things that aren't important anyway.

"Now count to ten."

"...nine, ten..."

"Oh, Eleonore," she cries. "I don't, I don't believe it. You really remembered. It's beautiful. Really beautiful," and I get a giant hug. The watch has coloured moons and stars set into the face, and a little box for the day and the date, and I don't tell her that it is likely her Uncle Paul that has probably influenced Papi's generosity, especially after their disappearing act at my party. They are now truly friends. Papi thinks the Nazis are going to stop all Jewish newspapers, so he's hoping in turn that we can have Paul's after he has finished with them. The Germans wouldn't dare interfere with their reading, of course, because there's nothing a Dutchman likes more than to devour his paper with a morning coffee. And they still are doing their very best to try and keep the Dutch people onside.

Chapter 8

"It's elementary, my dear Watson," except it's not. Far from it. Eleonore has told me about the secret of the zoo, and I have been puzzling over it ever since. So how would the English detective set about this?

An innocent explanation. A speck of dust on the lens, and the refraction of sunlight.

Another: A zookeeper takes to peering at the crowd.

A not-so-innocent explanation. A fugitive. But from what? And at great risk, surely?

Another: A fugitive known to the zookeepers. But wouldn't that be dangerous?

More than one fugitive? Frankly, this doesn't help. Round and round it goes in my head, and then a moment of clarity. Is it at all possible? Can a human live alongside wolves? And survive? And there's one person, at least in our circle, who is certain to know the answer. He hasn't paid much attention to me of late. And he might also know more about that shiny metal object hanging at the entrance to Eleonore's apartment.

October 1940

I have persuaded Freyja never to say 'Germans' again. We have been calling them 'Boots' for a good while now, but it will always be 'Nazi' from now on. It will be harder for her, I know, because one of the things she likes in me is the funny way I pronounce things, which is unlike any other person she has ever met and she explains to everyone "is just like a German" even though that is what I am! But we have to face the facts. At first, the Nazis pretended that they were welcome here and that they would definitely stop us from having a revolution like in Russia where, if you had money, they would kill you and steal it. But they have just been tricking us all along. Today we are told we must never go to a restaurant or a hotel again. But why? When Papi is travelling and has found a nice part of the country, we sometimes get to stay nearby whilst he is visiting the watch shops. And now every Nazi soldier in Holland, and not just the ones at the very top, must have been told the new rules, so they can no longer say they don't know what is going on. Freyja goes to Uncle Paul's and Aunt Myrese's house to listen to the secret broadcasts from England, which are also banned, so it's not just our families they hate. The only good thing that is happening right now, quite often in the night, is the steady drone of engines in the giant aeroplane above us just like black vultures which Mama says are on their way to teach Hitler a lesson that he won't forget.

Oh, and Moeder will also allow us to have 'two' Hanukahs this year. Although the Dutch Christmas is only a couple of days, if you add Hanukah in, it means gifts and celebrations going on forever. And perhaps she'll even let us have a tree? I've never had a tree.

At least that's cleared up. Dirk says there are many stories of wolves and humans living alongside the other. In a zoo (although I haven't told him about my discovery, of course) the animals do not need to hunt for food, or to seek territory, or suffer from predators, so many of their natural instincts are suppressed. And they are used to the presence of their keepers. So if a large shelter did exist within the wolf mountain, they would be no more curious than normal. In any case, wolves sleep a lot during the day. It would be only at night time that a fugitive would need caution, and then the zoo is closed, so they could walk about free. I suddenly have a picture in my head of people promenading around in the moonlight, just like the Englishman Lowry's stick pictures which Eleonore has in her father's art books. I sometimes wish my father was more like hers. I ask Papa if we could place a Mezuzah, which is what Dirk says the little object is called, on our door too, to show that we support Eleonore, but he only says why am I so ridiculous? You see, it's him now asking me the why question when it's Father who is ridiculous because the little parchment words in their silver box are taken from our Bible and help us to feel protected by God. Who wouldn't want that? So I shall call him Vader, and not Papa from now on. I think he will soon get the message.

November 1940

I am colder than I have ever been in the whole of my life. If Mamie had told me of Dutch winters, I would have never left Germany behind. You must have gloves, otherwise, your fingers will not stop tingling for hours, and layer after layer on top, though none of us has had anything new, except

Freyja's lovely warm cardigan of course, for ages and ages. But something curious has happened.

I had a letter from the zoo from Mr Armand asking if I would like to visit with Moeder and my cousins. Erin never stops talking about mermaids now, so Moeder has made her a long silky tail from an old nightdress which we took turns to paint, although the paint kept slipping off onto the carpet. I am amazed that he remembers that I was disappointed not to see the reptile house, and he knows how much Erin loved the aquarium. "As a budding artist too," he writes, "we know that you would want to see some of the pictures on display." I am ashamed I mentioned my passion for art, as it's not that I am Van Gogh or anything, so I had to mug up with Papa's books. He added a postscript. "Why not keep it a secret from Freyja?" Which is another grown-up mystery I will have to puzzle over.

We are asked to wait at the entrance at 4 o'clock, which is quite late, as it is getting dark at this time of year around teatime. Moeder has put on her smartest winter coat, with fur trim and winter boots, and lots of colourful scarves, so she looks just like a Hollywood film star, "I always was a classy dresser," she says to the cousins, but all Erin wants to know is "What is that icicle dripping from your nose," when we venture out. In fact, icicles are everywhere. They drop like daggers from the window boxes and the pretty scalloped roofs and I wonder if this wouldn't be the worst way to die. A stab through the heart. But then we are so busy being careful not to skid on the sparkling cobbles that the thought goes right out of my mind.

It isn't Mr Armand waiting for us at the gate, but a keeper who asks to be called Gert. I thought it strange that Freyja wasn't here, but I hadn't wanted to boast about the letter. Anyway, he is so funny with the little ones.

"It won't be long before all those people queuing over there won't bother paying. They'll be so skinny they'll squeeze through the fencing," he says, before picking up Reuben and giving him a little try, shoving, twisting and pushing against the rails. Now Reuben is only three years younger than me, so it's not ever going to work.

"We're visiting here first of all, Eleonore, so we don't bore the little ones too much," as we enter the gallery, and then, to Erin, "Wouldn't it be nicer if they were fish pictures though?"

"I can already draw fish pictures," she says, and Gert doesn't have a reply, which I believe means that he doesn't have any children of his own.

"And what about you, Reuben, what do you draw?"

He is a little bit shy, so Moeder says, "He loves dragons and snakes and creepy things." But Reuben remains tongue-tied.

"So Reuben. What say you that we go and visit a baby dragon house next?" and his little eyes light up.

"I'm not a great fan of paintings myself," says Gert, as we survey the battle scenes, which the label says are painted by Pieneman, and the landscapes of Kruseman. Reuben 'isn't scared' by all the rifles and smoke and cannons of the tiny red-coated men, but not a single still life for me to copy. I concentrate on the details instead and Moeder likewise, so I hardly catch what Gert is saying, except what is the best thing about fish? He has taken them to one side and they are sitting on his knee. The little ones are taking turns in guessing; for Erin, their translucent colours and bendy shapes, and Reuben their silky slithery movements. And then Gert adds, "The very best thing about fish, the very best thing, is that they live beneath the water, mostly out of harm's way."

At which Moeder observes, "So I'm glad no-one's told them about angling Gert," and they smile and share one of those grown-up knowing looks. I think Moeder quite likes Gert with his directness and tender way with the little ones. "Just think about it, Erin. If you were a fish and Reuben was trying to find you, tell me. Where would you hide? Remember; Reuben is a fish too,"

She gives it some thought. "The very best thing would be to find a big rock."

And Gert says, "But what about all the little pebbles and the deep gullies?"

Reuben hasn't entirely lost his tongue. "But Erin's far too big to hide with the fishes." Which, of course, makes perfect sense to Reuben.

The reptile house is a big disappointment to the little ones. For a start, it's far too dark and they get frightened that they will get lost, so Moeder takes them to buy some candy and I am lucky to have Gert all to myself. When I was small, my parents bought me a glass box to keep my terrapins and I could have it in my bedroom as long as I kept everything clean. I would give them imaginary names and plot elaborate journeys for them through impenetrable barriers until they were rescued. Gert asks me about school and, like all adults, he wants to know what I want to be when I grow up. Although it's 'doctor' or a 'lawyer' to my parent's friends. I am confident enough to chance my arm. "Well. After the last visit to the zoo, I have been wondering what kind of work there is to do with animals. Of a more scientific kind," which I remembered Mr Sunier saying. And then, because I am embarrassed, "Anyway. I've never asked what you do here, Gert?"

"Oh. Nothing particularly special, Eleonore. Not at all. What's a keeper? Perhaps the lowest species of all."

"But surely all the different jobs are important, aren't they? For instance, if you weren't here…" A long silence.

"If I weren't here, Eleonore, the wolves wouldn't have an easy time of it, would they?" My blood froze. What does he know of our secret? And if it's his secret too? I wanted to be out of there. And quickly.

We meet Moeder and the little ones by the candy store. They are holding huge sugary spirals of reds, green, blues; every colour under the sun, except Moeder, who believes she is health-conscious and is clutching the remnants of an apple. It's getting colder and darker now, and there are fewer and fewer people milling around us, so Gert hurries us to the aquarium. Of course, the baby dolphins entrance them, as do the sweeps of tiny fish of every hue. The ray fish is most worrying because they see it as a giant shark. And now, what next? It must be getting late and, well, Erin and Reuben are getting restless, their toes are icy, and they can see their breath forming little clouds ahead of them, so Gert says, "Just one last thing before I see you home." See us home? Moeder told him we lived very close to the zoo, but "I can't see you young ladies and gents alone on the streets. Besides, that's what Mr Sunier would want. And I know you like lions and tigers, Reuben. So what other animals like lions and tigers can you tell me about?"

Something just tells me where we might be heading next. Through the thin evening light, I spot the wolves' enclosure, eerily shadowed. We stop. "Now why don't you all stand there and hold hands, and we will see what they are having for their tea today." Gert lifts a wide plank, expertly crosses the moat towards the wolves and calls back, "Now, don't any of you be afraid. The wolves are my special friends, and I have been to visit their favourite butcher's shop." At that, he lifts a large trapdoor with its ring, which conceals a storage area beneath the ground, takes out a large grapple tool, and hooks up huge glistening bones of meat. Erin shivers and shakes, but I hold her hand all the tighter. Gert lays the bones on the very edge of the moat. "Just think," he said. "When the Germans starve us out, all you will need is a long stick and a nail."

Chapter 9

My favourite – the weekly cooking class, but far from normal. "In these days, we and our families must get used to living within our means," says our Principal. We don't see her very often because of the important work she has to do, but this lesson is when she 'keeps her hand in'. Today it's all about Dutch apple tart, which, as everyone knows, is the most famous sweet treat in our country. You just must serve it with thick cream, but 'Miss' as we must call her (no first names – for fairness she says), has a disappointment in store. "We are using substitute ingredients today, to preserve all the good things that we have for our long winter."

At this, Dirk, who has kindly swapped places with Eleonore for the lesson, whispers, "It's really because the Germans are stealing everything from us." I worry she doesn't think that I prefer him for changing places; it's just that I find it hard to lift the cast-iron pans, and he always likes to 'play the gentleman'. So today we are to replace all the normal things with powdered milk, and powdered eggs, margarine instead of butter, and the juice from some stewing apples to make everything runny and sweet, rather than sugar. That's the one good thing. There are still plenty of apples on the trees. They're almost the only abundant things left.

Cooking is quite a relief from this morning's lesson, and we are allowed to work at our own speed, so if you don't understand instructions or are especially clumsy, then it doesn't really matter.

But I still can't get out of my mind the guest who had visited earlier this morning. He's a little bit scary as he is very tall, has on a black shirt and trousers and shoes, and looks just like a scarecrow's shadow in the half-light cast by the blinds. He spoke to the whole school in the Main Hall. We had to stand and stay completely silent whilst he told us about the greatest exploits in Dutch history, such as William of Orange who defeated the Spanish, and Admiral Michiel de Ruyter who defended the Low Countries from its enemies. There were lots and lots more names, and we were all bored, but it all came down to Dutch spirit and pride and honour and other words that sound important, but no one knows quite what they mean. As soon as I got home that day, I telephoned Aunt Myrese. She said Uncle Paul, who takes an interest in these things, was still at work, but that this man was a Nazi, which surprised me because he was obviously Dutch. She asks when I might visit, but definitely not with my parents, I think. I really hope that they will become better friends; after all, Paul is Moeder's brother.

December 1940

We are in the 'den' area of the school which is known as the 'survival' area because Montessori ideas believe we should live much simpler lives, and if we can't even manage a place for shelter, what about facing the bigger questions in life? This is near to where the chickens are kept and where

Freyja and I come to collect the eggs, which we hatch out in the classroom so we can learn all about their biology, watch their little hearts beat and count and measure things about them as they grow. It is a tight fit in here because ours has just enough room for two.

"I think we should tell someone about the zoo, Freyja."

"Someone?"

"Someone in authority, Freyja."

"But why should we? It was you who saw the man anyway."

"And I shared the secret, Freyja. So you are in it as much as me. Something terrible might be happening and people could get hurt. They might even close it down."

"I don't believe this, Eleonore. Coming from you. Why would you even think of it?"

"I'm thinking of it because we all have a duty. To our country."

"You sound as crazy as that man in uniform. You aren't even Dutch."

"I'm going to tell anyway."

"And you might get us into trouble, Eleonore. For not telling before."

"I've written it all in my diary and the names of the important people we have met there. And yours too. I'll show them the diary."

"You're horrible, really horrible."

"And you're a crybaby. It won't make any difference."

I can't believe what I'm hearing.

"Well then. I'll make you cry. I know why you're doing this…Because you're sneaky and sly. Not what you pretend to be. Just like all the rest."

"What do you mean?"

"Are they giving you a reward? Admit it. Perhaps they'll leave you alone if you tell on someone? Is that what you think?" Silence.

"So why are you looking at me like that?"

"Because you're so angry. I can tell, Freyja. So stop it. Stop it now. I need to explain something."

"I won't listen. I really won't. Just find another friend."

"Freyja. Please, Just for a minute. Listen. Not everything is what you think."

"Whatever you say. It won't make it any better."

"If I tell you it was all a test… Only a test. You must believe me. And I'm sorry, so sorry to upset you."

"You know what? You've made me sadder than I've ever been, Eleonore. I never thought you could…"

"Look. Give me your hand. I think you are the best person in the whole world. The very best person. But sometimes you're too nice for your own good. And you have to understand me. Every minute now, there are people in great fear. You can't ever know what it's like to be called names, humiliated and betrayed. Even by your neighbours and acquaintances, for there are rotten Dutch people out there who do pay for names. Do you know why I can't ask you to visit us now? Because the Nazis have placed soldiers on the bridge to make it difficult for people to come and go."

"But why did you need to be so cruel?"

"We have a secret, Freyja. And it might be a very dangerous secret. It might only seem to be about a zoo but I want you to know how hard it is to keep secrets, and how it feels when they threaten you. Here, here. Take my hand, now."

"Spread my fingers. Just like this, Freyja, right across your face and your eyes."

"I will. If you will do the same."

"I'll do the same. Watch me. Do you remember Mr Sunnier? He had this phrase. 'Till the end of time,' which I couldn't get out of my mind. I want us to swear it. That we will never betray our secret. Ever, 'Till the end of time.'"

"Till the end of time."

Now I am crying too.

Chapter 10

I don't know if I can forgive Eleonore for what she did, but the more I think about it, the more I understand. She wants me to feel what she's going through, and also how important it is to stay true to another person, come what may. And never ever to betray them. I sobbed myself to sleep that first night but awoke feeling dreadful because of how good is our life compared to others. And also, how did those cruel words come into my head? We must always look out for the best in others, I decide. And though Father can be a dreadful pain sometimes, he has lots of good points. Moeder tells me in confidence that he sometimes 'helps out' Uncle Paul and Aunt Myrese, which I suppose means money, but she wouldn't go any further. And he drove me there in our motorcar when I went over to their house 'to discuss things'; things being the strange uniformed man who came to school.

"You have to know that we Dutch have our Nazis too, Freyja. They belong to a party called the NSB. You can't always spot them, and some don't even wear uniforms and live in perfectly normal homes."

"But why do they do it? What's wrong with them?"

"Well. That's a tricky question, and I'm not sure if I have all the answers. Nor even many of the answers. But between us, we'll have to try."

"Suppose you have a nice house and family and a good business," says Myrese, "and the future looks rosy so you can always plan for tomorrow. Maybe to have a family. And you can afford good food and trips to the parks and museums and really everything you could desire. And then it all goes away. How would you feel?"

"I can understand that I suppose, but how can things change for the worse so quickly?"

"Think about Holland today, Freyja. We can't buy so much from the shops or light our fires so often and travel so easily. When you think about it, we're having to share soap. Could you ever dream that? And why? Because something big, something which we didn't expect, has made a change. And these things, like wars, or collapse of money, make people scared."

"But still…"

"So perhaps they want someone powerful to lead them and show them a way out, who can't be easily got rid of, and perhaps can blame someone else for misfortune, and then things will go back to how they used to be. That's why they like the flags and the uniforms and the booming voices; they have their big strong bully at last. But this time he's on their side."

"And there are some people," says Myrese, "who've never had much, and have been envious of the nice house and expensive things and who get promised they will get that too."

"But Vader calls that communism," I say. I am rather pleased with that remark because it shows that I too can think in grown-up ways, and grown-up thinking helps other people think too. Of course, we talked about lots of other things, not so serious things, and what Saint Nicholas, dressed in his red robes and riding on a horse, might bring me for Christmas. And because Uncle Paul had told me all about Hanukkah, I needed ideas for a lot of little presents for Eleonore. He's the wisest person I know, is Paul; he also told me the Jewish children aren't allowed to spend money on Saturday, their Sabbath, which is why they buy their zoo tickets on Fridays. So our English detective will not need to help with that one. I love that my uncle has twinkly eyes and says funny things as well as a clever mind and that Aunt Myrese puts her boots up on the sofa, and when we sit down to eat, all our food comes together at the same time, and there are no rules about eating up and conversation, which means we are often talking at the same time. The food they especially like, which is colourful and spicy, comes from one of our colonies, which Uncle Paul tells us we've invaded, and here we go again. Grown-ups! Myrese especially doesn't like Paul's 'colony voice' which he imitates to describe the food from Indonesia, but then again he does another voice for people from the south of Holland whom he calls "Bantu" like the Dutch in Africa, so I suppose it evens out in the end. So it's not just Nazis, but the colonies they don't like, and at that moment, I think I would like to spend my whole life studying disagreeing, but how on earth would you know which side to be on?

January 1941

I believe that we have had the last good Hanukkah for a long time. We lit the candles and shared the gifts with our friends, but I know how worried everyone is about day-to-day things like finding food and fuel. We are having to "eek out" as Mamie puts it. If someone is lucky enough to get to the bakers in time for the last loaf, they will always share, and I loved it that Freyja's family invited me to Sinterklaas night and to help with the tree and to swap presents. So things aren't altogether bleak. I think that she and I have forgiven each other and when I told Father about our fall out, and bad things said and done, but not about the zoo, of course, he said that "you need to learn when it is important to be tough and when to be tender." There are more and more bad things by the day, though. All the Jewish people have had to register with the Nazis, and they say it is to help make sure there is adequate provision for everyone, but you can't believe a word they say. Why else would they put a fence around the Jewish area in Jodenbuurt? And now here is a new sign at our zoo, "No Jews admitted." Freyja can't believe it, but she tells me, her moeder says, "Don't worry. Mr Sunier plays a clever game." and I'm pleased that I am finally getting the hang of these grown-up sayings at long last.

Chapter 11

Four or five sharp bangs at the door, as if with a rifle-butt. Lots of angry men's voices. Mama lifting me from my bed as if I am a child. It still feels like nighttime. I am so frightened I am trembling uncontrollably. Mama, Papa, and I have to stand against the bedroom wall. Three or four Nazi soldiers with shiny belt buckles, and pistols, which is all I remember, because the men are as big as giants, looking under beds, asking where is the attic and two Dutchmen in long coats pretending to be polite and saying, "such things are sometimes necessary." I am not stupid; they are opening drawers and cupboards and looking amongst clothes and papers, so it is more than just a person they are searching for. A neighbour knocking to ask if we are okay and our Dutchman answering "Everything is under control, madam." Always polite, as if this is normal. And feeling ashamed for my parents that they too, do not have a weapon or even fists to defend their family, which is what all parents will want to do. Time feels endless, and I do not understand what the soldiers are shouting at each other. Is it about the zoo? Is this how Eleonore feels often? But now they seem satisfied, and the man in a coat hands Papa a form which says that no harm or damage was done to any of us, which he has to sign. And he thanks us and walks away with his soldiers through the scattered papers, the bedding and the clothes strewn everywhere. And I am sad for Papa because this time I know that even he hasn't a single answer to the 'why' question.

"Eleonore. We're only allowed five minutes."

"I can't hear you very well, Freyja."

"Then I'll shout. Can I tell you what happened to us?"

(The person watching me in the mirror is angry)

"Is it horrible, Freyja?"

"It is horrible."

"Well, don't tell me then."

"Eleonore! It really was very horrible. Don't be so cruel."

"I'm only joking. Tell me. What happened?"

"We had Nazi soldiers in the house."

"In your house? Why?"

"We don't know, but I was shaking so much I was nearly sick."

(I check in the mirror to see if I'm alright now)

"You get sick so easily. Even a ride in your papa's…"

"Stop it, Eleonore. This really is serious."

"Is it about our secret?"

"How could they know? They wouldn't even talk to us. But I kept a picture of you in my head just to give me courage."

"That's so brave. Thank you."

"But I think we're safe now, Eleonore, thank goodness. But I've been thinking. I have a question."

"A why question?"

"Do you think we really understand danger? I mean, like real grown-ups feel it? Is it much worse for them? Yes I know.

70

We know danger's there too. All around us. Like crossing in front of the trams. But how is it for them?"

"That's why you should study thinking, Freyja. When I'm busy being a scientist, or a doctor or lawyer, you could help everybody think. Like Spinoza, or whatever he's called."

"Uncle Paul's the thinker in our family. I think I might ask him."

"What about?"

"Eleonore. You've forgotten already. About what the Nazis just did."

"Freyja. Would you like to go to the zoo again? We could use our pass, and then the grown-ups wouldn't get in the way."

February 1941

We can take courage. The streets in Amsterdam are decked with flowers of every colour; workers flags are flying, thousands of brave people gather. Drifts of rich tobacco smoke, roasting coffee, wafts of frying fish. After all, angry people are hungry people too – and the occasional stench from the fetid canals always lingering. Freyja comes with us, with her aunt and uncle and their gaudily dressed actor and musician friends, and it seems as if the whole world is on our side. Brass bands play and speakers speak, their voices fading and re-emerging amidst the raucous atmosphere, and though I cannot always understand, I know that they are speaking with passion. And here and there the coffeehouses and bars are doing great business with cries of 'Proost Heineken' because some say they are supporting the protest by providing beer. My heart leaps to see Papi and Mamie so happy after

71

weeks of glum shrugs. It is a holiday atmosphere until the grey trucks begin to move in and the rifles and the dogs and the brutes emerge, corralling the crowds this way and that, splitting up friends and family, ordering hands above heads. But the people are brave and defiant, and today nothing will move them too far away. Then again, if the Poles couldn't stop them, and the Danes and the Norwegians couldn't, what hope have we people in a small country, without rifles and lacking evil intent?

Chapter 12

No one has seen Uncle Paul for days, and everyone is at their wit's end. At first, Aunt Myrese says not to worry; after all, these are artistic people who frequently drink, and talk and argue and even fight into the night, until it's too late and long past the curfew and they must grab a sofa or thick blanket to sleep just where they are. Also, some have false papers with disguised names, which do not appear on the lists of communist or liberal democrat members or others the Nazis hate. It was Uncle Paul who had explained that Nazis believe that if you are not with them, then you must be against them, and to be with them you have to know that, if you love a person who is of the same sex, or you don't have 'pure blood' as they say is true of the Jews and gipsies, or that people should not always be good followers but should question, then you are an enemy. I am missing Uncle Paul more than I can say. Is it possible to even think that I might love him over Father? But Aunt Myrese came to stay, and we will visit all the police stations, in turn, to ask if they have news of Paul, and will they tell us if they have, and because we believe that most Dutch policemen are good in heart, we know they will.

We girls are allowed to return to the zoo as long as our moeder's deliver and collect us. We agree on three hours, which should be plenty of time, and besides, we have our watches, and we ask at the window, by the sign 'Jews not Allowed', for Gert, and the lady says he is busy, but she will send a message. She finds us two tiny stools as if we are still children, but it's better than standing in the cold. We watch the queue carefully. I know it is silly, but we might catch a fleeting glimpse, and I have described Paul to Eleonore so that she can play detective, too. But now it's not a game anymore, it really is real. So whilst I sit, I think. As you grow older, I'm sure you notice more and more about people and sights and things; it's as if the numerous little dabs of paint become one, and make the complete picture. Now that it is spring, and perhaps soon to warm up, Amsterdam is awash with a whole suite of smells, of nutmeg, cloves, pepper, vanilla and cinnamon and not just the usual drying fats and cheese. So it's no longer just the pretty rucking and ribbons around Eleonore's party dress to be seen, but the woollen stockings of the hurrying women, the boots, the coats with furs and stoles, the hats, featherless or not. And nowadays the general thinness and shabbiness of the people, which strikes me perhaps for the very first time. And fewer and fewer bicycles, which the Nazis wish to have for themselves. But so far, no sign of Paul.

Gert arrives, all smiling and bluster and "What are your plans for today, ladies?" which makes us feel very grown-up. And then "Mind you. I do have some work to do." And so, to be grown-up too, Eleonore says, "In which case, let's see what else keeps you busy; apart from the wolves that is," with a mischievous glance.

As we walk, "You saw the sign at the entrance, did you? Isn't it funny that we are surrounded by lots of dangerous wild animals, but they want us to keep out civilised human beings," and I understand that lovely Gert is much more than a lowly zookeeper.

"In my job you need to know where we keep all the essential supplies," he says as we enter a vast sweet-sickly warehouse with mountains of hay, hundreds of grubby-looking sugar beets, swede, and beetroots scattered around, and it is a mystery to us that, at home, we can only have small amounts of butter, milk and little meat and bread, which runs out quickly in the shops anyway, yet Gert can feed an entire army with his supplies.

"The Director has a little deal with the Germans," he says. "On cold days they come and hang around the giant steamers that boil up the potatoes and yams and vegetables, and scraps of meat, and when the cooks leave for a cigarette…You get my drift?" He probably does realise that growing up means getting more and more keys to their adult codes. "You know something? We did the Germans a great favour in finding a use for all those dead horses after the bombing in Rotterdam." This was something that I could have done without knowing, but Gert is a man who speaks his mind, and who couldn't forgive him?

Next, we help him load bundles of hay into a large wheeled container, which means we get to see the animal enclosures where the haylofts are located. The giraffes' necks mean long ladders to climb, but you could imagine Gert is more likely attempting to sell us apartments. "Lovely accommodation, girls, nice and snug, decent sizes, but lacking bathroom facilities. I can do this one for only 500 guilders. Or if you'd like to knock me down?" Much lower located are the deer and the donkey feeds, and though we are getting itchy eyes and runny noses, we are getting the best ever zoo tour yet. And then he's no longer talking zoos, but pointing to a brick-built building glimpsed beyond the top of the boundary fence. "You live in there too, Eleonore." She's mystified, but he goes on. "You want to know what happens to those forms your parents must fill in? They are copied to index cards and stored so that the Nazis can keep an eye on you." She doesn't quite know whether to believe him or not – it's very much like those children's stories of the Big Bad Wolf. And why would he want to frighten her anyway?

It's getting time to leave, so we wander back to the exit, Gert is being strangely silent as we pass the wolves' enclosure. As we say goodbye, he says, "How's your drawing, Eleonore?"

She's surprised but, as she's always polite and modest, she answers, "I'll try."

And then Gert says, "Try drawing a map of the whole of Artis from memory, and then you can show me the next time you visit." It's as if they are sharing a secret.

March 1941

Things at school are not as they were. From time to time, a friend does not return and no one knows why. Even our favourite teacher, Miss Kelter, hasn't been here for a week and we miss her rushing around the place, never still. She has always made me think of a windmill, what with her whirling arms like sails, and her strong trunk. But then her sweet smile makes her a person once again, and there she is, everywhere at once, holding steady a chalking slate, retrieving a dropped pencil, wiping a little one's nose. We see much more of our

Principal now, who wants to keep us calm and has explained that with things as they are, she isn't always given the money to run the school properly, but she will always do her best. Often the tram runs out of power or the road has been suddenly blocked, so we arrive late. So now she tells us that it's our turn to lend a hand. Surely we are old enough to help with the little ones? So from time to time, we take it, in turn, to walk them to the annexe, Freyja for storytelling, as she is a very good reader, and me for art, which is really only colouring in until they can hold their crayons properly. I think this would please Mrs Montessori, as she could see no reason for grown-ups to tell children everything, because who knows better than a child what only children know? And Dirk seems to have found another girlfriend, so all is good on that front. PS: In any case, Freyja says she never kissed him. Not even once.

Chapter 13

Everyone is so happy. Uncle Paul is safe again. Myrese brings the news, and of course, we are all curious as to what has happened. Myrese says he has been "having a little talk with the Nazis," which, of course, is grown-up code, and I am certain that it would have been them and not Paul, who did the talking. Which might explain why he is not here and 'just resting'. She tells us he was asked for his identity papers and the soldier saw that under 'Occupation' was written 'actor' and Paul was a little bit nervous and so as the soldier said he liked movies, they chatted together and what was his favourite of all time? The Nazis wanted to know where Paul acted as well, and Paul thought that was an end to it. Until sometime later, when the soldiers piled out of a truck and burst down the stairs into the rehearsal room and discovered a printing press. The one who held Paul's neck down tight against the cold inky metal plate didn't believe it was only used for preparing flyers for their shows, and then tighter still because he and his friends were "fighting and dying for freedom, whilst you and your Nancy friends are prancing around in powder and wigs" or something which I didn't really understand and didn't even ask. And they also want to know the names and addresses of his family and friends.

March 1941

All the colour has been drained out of Amsterdam. The flowers and banners of the February protest (which was an expression of the anger of the good people of the city against the Nazis who had begun to take away those they did not like) have been long swept away. Freyja says every year around December, all Dutch children are taught to wonder whether Santa Claus might take them away for being bad until you realise that this is the best trick ever for keeping you good, so why would you take the good children who should receive presents instead? Freyja has given us the news about her uncle, and so Papi asks, "Why don't we all meet up and celebrate, and see how things are?" And after a moment's thought; "And where better than the flower market, and you could bring your bikes?" When the Nazis first came, there were coloured postcards of soldiers standing in front of Flower Mountains of every shape, and vivid reds yellows tangerines, and greens, and garden bulbs the size of turnips all carefully arranged on the floating stalls, so the world would know they came only for peace. Nowadays, most of us cross the street when we see the boots.

It's a lovely spring day when we set off, and Papi has strapped his large black valise to the seat rest at the back of the cycle, which usually means business. The streets are largely empty of cars, but everywhere you have to dodge and swerve the mobile gun carriages, the armoured cars, tack around the cement blocks and barbed wire, curse the incessant barking of the Alsatians, which I know Dirk would like because they are like wolves. Then, irritated, "Why is it that I am still thinking about Dirk? He's not even my boyfriend."

It's a disappointment to see that there's only Freyja and Paul there. I really do like her moeder now that I'm more grown-up, because she's not so much the frightened mouse when her father is not around, and she has a hiccupy, happy giggle just like a girl that sometimes can't stop. And if only she wore the clothes my mother favours…!

Papi is overjoyed to see his old friend once more, and they hug and squeeze until they have to break off for their schnapps. And we get double helpings of real lemonade sold at the citrus stall. Of course, the story of the arrest is swiftly told, and when Freyja gets overexcited and joins in the story of nancies and prancers, she says, 'Papa Paul' by mistake.

"And now we grown-ups must get down to work," he says, and we haven't a clue what he means except that it means only one thing when said in front of children, and it is a code for telling us to leave them alone for a while.

We have to push our cycles as often as we can ride them because everywhere is an obstacle course. A tall tower, like a water tower, with scary guns pointing skyward, looms by the Market. It's to shoot down the British planes, who don't oblige because they fly too high. The canals have soldiers at the bridges, but no matter, we are too young to carry identity cards. Though not everything has changed. The buzz of motorboats on the water, the terraces and green spaces, once overflowing with people who now have less to spend on their beers and ice cream, the shrieking trams and squealing seagulls. They are the same. But there aren't so many young men anymore, because the Nazis force them to do 'essential labour', which really means essential to the Nazis, and they must be taken away to Germany. And underneath, there is an eerie silence, despite the clanking of motorised vehicles, the boots and the dogs; there is no 'music'. No excitable drifts of cafe and bar talk, no hurdy-gurdy or accordion trills, no casual conversations on street corners. The Nazis have killed it all. And, because of the street obstacles, we miss, most of all, the thing all good Amsterdammer cyclists do as naturally as breathing, that swoop of heart and nerve you get from speeding down the canal sides, neglecting both bell and brakes. When we get back to Papi, I notice that he no longer has his valise.

Chapter 14

Eleonore thinks that Dirk no longer likes me, but I don't tell her a single thing. At school, he's no different from any other boy, but has she forgotten about church? It's Sunday and it's cold in here, and it's the story of 'Noah and the flood' again, but now at least we are sitting away from our parents. I can see Dirk's father, his wispy strands of hair showing clear against a shiny bald head so that each time he makes a half-glance, it shuffles apart. A Dutch child knows every word of Noah's story because we are forever told, "We live under the sea." Not strictly speaking, of course, but without our dams and canals to control the water, we really would. 'And after 40 days' and then 'another seven days' and 'the raven', and the dove returning with a twig which means the water has likely gone away, and the rainbow to show that never-never again...and the Reverend drones on. And I am thinking, will Dirk and I get any time together after church, because I have been reading the adventures of Mowgli, in my Kipling book, the Indian boy raised by wolves, and how the wolves remain friends and protect him and each other, and that reason always triumphs over brute force, as in Spinoza, until another thought skips into my mind. "What if Amsterdam were one giant ark and we could gather together all the good people and sail away to the land of…?" It would be a shame about the animals though. We might have to leave them behind, and, in any event, where on earth could we go? And then there is the little matter of finding the boat. It gets complicated.

April 1941

Papi finally got me 'the Hound of the Baskervilles,' about the English detective, Sherlock Holmes. We looked at all his books and decided that this one might suit Dirk too. The important thing is clues, and it has given me a big idea for my drawing for Gert, the wolf keeper. I'm so excited I want to tell Freyja right away, but they have taken away our telephone now, so it will just have to wait for a school day. But before that, it will take at least another visit to the zoo.

Our parents trust us more now that we are older, so we can take the tram ourselves, as long as we are back straight after closing time. It is important we see the zoo at dusk and do not give anything away to Gert. Freyja will pack a large tape measure in with the food snacks, and I need an assortment of coloured pencils and squared paper. It will be a long afternoon so we need to be here early.

Gert is thrilled to see us and asks, "What can I show you today, ladies?" but he's quite happy we want to explore alone. We don't tell that we have already "stepped out" the whole zoo perimeter, and marked the number of steps onto our plan. "Now, take your tape, Freyja, and measure only the largest gaps in the railings."

"Not until you tell me what's this about," she says.

And I say, "have I ever broken a promise, and you'll find out soon enough," so she measures and I mark. It all takes far longer than we thought, so we ask if we can sit down with Gert to eat our sandwiches. "Moeder makes our own German bread," I tell him, "but it is too dry without butter."

"Not to worry," he replies, "there are plenty of ducks who'll help you eat it," and his jokes always make us laugh. Lucky that Freyja has lots of cheese biscuits and boiled eggs and apples from the trees behind their house, and she always comes to my rescue.

Gert asks about progress on my map so I say, "Gert, do you have a visitor guide? And can we borrow it for now? I promise I won't cheat. It will be my plan and mine alone."

As he goes to his office, Freyja whispers, "What is going on, Eleonore, for goodness' sake?"

And I remind her, "Remember Freyja. We're playing the detective, and these things take a lot of time," so we button our lips.

Now it's time for our stakeout. "Just show the paths to the places we already know, Freyja," and we squat down together whilst we shade the routes to the wolf enclosure, the moats, the canteen, the food stores, the giraffe and deer and donkey houses. I will add in the strange low-roofed brick building that keeps my secret later.

By now, she's bursting with frustration that she is not in on my plan and suddenly she stands straight up, sits on a bench and point blank refuses to go any further.

"Not a single step."

"I can see you'll burst, so I'll tell you, Freyja. But, don't forget the 'Till the end of time' promise?" and we hook our little fingers as we did that day on the market.

"Promise."

"Do you remember the very first time we came to the zoo, together with Mama and Dirk and your cousins?"

"And you saw the wolf-man," she says.

"Ever since, I've thought that the zoo is telling us something. Mr Armand, for instance, and his telling of the fish hiding beneath the water."

"They weren't hiding, Eleonore. That's where fish live."

"But it's the way he said it. And then Gert and Reuben at the railings, and the meat store. It's too much of a coincidence."

"And you think you're really as smart as our detective, Eleonore? He always has to prove things."

"So why did we see the food store and the canteens? You tell me."

"Couldn't we ask him?"

"Who?"

"Ask Gert?"

"If I've guessed right, how could he tell? He would put everyone in danger, Freyja, and himself."

It seems as if there is nowhere else to go with this.

"So, what do you suggest we do?"

"We find a long stick and walk right around the moat. Right around, and find the deep spots and the shallow spots. And mark them."

"This is not elementary, my Dear Watson," Freyja says.

That's just showing off because she knows lots more about Sherlock Holmes than me.

I'm firm. "Just do it, Freyja. Just do it."

We have a family truce because Papa has invited Uncle Paul and Aunty Myrese over to 'clear the air', and I must be there too, which means that they are really treating me as a grown-up now. They listen to the 'secret radio' from London, which is very brave because you can go to prison for it. And they must all be friends for now, because they have brought a treat of liquorish buttons for me, and flowers for my parents, and bringing gifts is a nice Dutch tradition.

Papa lays out a large map on the table and I have my pencils so that I can colour in. My job is to shade all the good countries who are 'The Allies' in orange, and all the bad countries, 'The Axis Powers', in red. Orange is the national colour of our country so that is sensible. Aunt Myrese tells us what they have been learning from the radio, that Britain is safe because her soldiers were rescued from France, and the Nazi air force was beaten in air battles. So that is all in orange. Some countries can't have colour because they are not on anyone's side and Paul calls these "Neutral." Mamie tells me she will colour in all the countries that the Nazis have captured, like Norway and Belgium, and Poland and Hungary and France and...the list goes on. She's quicker than me, so I help do the Italian ones. I know that Mussolini, another Nazi, like Hitler, has joined in too, but now I am colouring Greece red and then Egypt and I realise just how terrible things could be. There is only one big country that could help us out and that is America and that is Neutral. Nearly the whole map is covered in red now, "like the English Empire of one hundred years ago," says Paul and "that was terrible too." although we haven't been taught anything about it at school so far. And then I look once more at the map and now I see that it's a sea of blood because all of those battles have left people dead and maimed and crippled, and children without their parents and their pain and distress and nightmares and finally Uncle Paul says, "Who will win then, Freyja? Who has the most pieces?"

He wants me to be grown-up and have an opinion, and me answering back "It's not a game of chess, Paul. No one ever wins in any war." They were all very quiet then, and when they said that they had difficult things to discuss, I knew they wanted me out of the way.

Later, I came to wave goodnight to our guests and it was then, as they left, that father turned and quietly said, "Freyja, my darling. I think it is better if you don't spend so much time with Eleonore now. Don't you?" And my heart exploded and I knew there was no point in asking why, and I cried and cried and cried and Papa put his arms around me and I could see he was crying too and he said. "You are more precious to us than anything in the world, Freyja; you have to believe that. But you must also trust me. You really must." I tugged myself away from him and fled upstairs.

May 1941

Papi has been trying to find some way to get us out of Holland before complete disaster strikes. There are some famous watchmakers in Switzerland, including a man who has invented a watch that you don't have to wind! It has a little moving ball inside so that every time the wrist moves, the watch spring is renewed. Genius. Mother says Papi has to be 'very discrete' about any move, which means we don't get to learn any details such as Who? When? And Where? But it does cheer me up. What else is there to smile about? I haven't had a new pair of shoes for a year or so and my toes pinch whenever we go out. You need a special card for clothes and shoes and that means having to show your identity, which I know will go straight to the place in the zoo. So why should we risk it?

The other thing is that my tummy rumbles day and night because now nothing can be brought in to Holland from outside, so there is no jelly, or dried fruits which we use a lot for our cakes, or coffee or jam or lard and there is not even the scent of baking bread. For the last weeks, Papi hasn't even gone to work and how could he? He left his valise of samples in the flower market with Freyja's uncle, which I told him was very silly at the time. And he just smiled, which I thought was even sillier. Now he has to rely on pictures to show his clients.

Chapter 15

I won't go to school until I discover the truth. They cannot force me, I know, and I don't really like to fall out with Moeder, because it is my father who has brought my life to a stop. I wonder whether he has somehow made Eleonore leave the Montessori, or will prevent me from going out without being supervised? I even think about running away to live with Uncle Paul and Aunt Myrese because I know they would have me, and not even tell. I am frightened I will lose the picture of my best ever friend that I always keep in my mind, and that it will fade away, just like our love for one another. How can grown-ups be so cruel and secretive when they tell us they love us to the moon and back?

It doesn't make any sense.

It is on the second day, there is a knock on the bedroom door. There, with her smiley face and eyes the colour of the deepest sea, stands Eleonore. "I am here to take you to school," she says in that funny strict German way and then she laughs and leaps on the bed and gives me the biggest hug of my whole life, and my mind is one enormous jumble, and I wonder if that's the same for Vader?

Of course, they can't keep us separate at school, but two more teachers have gone away, so we spend almost our entire day helping the little ones with their reading and writing and numbers in different rooms. The Catholic parents seem to be having more children by the week, which Dirk says is because they're not their real children, so another puzzle for Sherlock Holmes to fathom. We no longer have our canteen for lunch – it's an overflow annexe – and we must bring our own food to eat just where we are and I secretly share with Eleonore because Moeder says I must, and I want to anyway.

The biggest difference now is that Moeder comes to collect me from school each day and I don't know whether for my safety or to make sure I don't break my father's new rule.

June 1941

I don't know how to write this. A big hole has come into our lives. We got a letter from the authorities telling us we must move from our building and take only our essential furniture and things with us, and they will provide for us somewhere else. Not only us, but our friends too, and our cousins Reuben and Erin and their mummies and daddies and the whole of our familiar world. Papi says this is the time to stay strong – to have 'hairs on one's teeth' – but I don't know how I will bear it.

We are in a lorry, open at the back, but this time, with flaps for windows and hard rubber tyres which rumble the cobbles as we pass through a seeming dying city. There are no flowers in window boxes or brightly-coloured bicycles or oliebollen stalls, or people smartly dressed and the theatre lights are all off. I am in the back, with our few pieces of essential furniture and possessions, as there is a strict limit, and there's only just enough room in the cab for the driver and my parents. We are not the only ones; many are in lorries today, lined up in the street at dawn, just as the few people now in the streets line up to watch us, and no, it's not like Queen's Day where everyone is cheering the people and floats with their mountains of flowers and waving their orange hats and scarves. It's as if there's an overwhelming sadness.

The wind and dust are in my eyes, and I can't be sure whether it's that or that I am silently weeping. I think of Freyja and who could help, but my mind goes blank and I try over and over not to think and now, ahead, I see the long wire fence stretching seemingly into the distance, and I know exactly what they want to do with us.

It was the saddest day when Eleonore told me her story. To cheer her up, I said, "Never mind. You live right by the zoo now. You'll be able to visit every day," but I knew I had said the wrong thing straightaway when her eyes watered, so I had to hold her tight and say, "I'm so sorry, Eleonore. The world has gone crazy and cruel and it's not fair," and we stayed like that, tight together, for a long time, and I learned that there are times when it is better just to say nothing at all.

There have been lots of new buildings at the school. They have taken away our little 'survival' area and built giant metal shelters which are there for when the 'nasty allies', the ones painted in orange, invade our country. That's what's said in Uncle Paul's newspaper (which I pass on every week to Eleonore) because really, it says, their fighting is all about "getting their bits of Africa and Europe back again." If I do get to study 'arguing' one day, which aunt Myrese says is called philosophy, I imagine I'll be clearer about these things.

I wish I hadn't mentioned the zoo, because I know Eleonore will want us to visit when things settle down, and what will I tell her? That I am banned from seeing her outside of school? I can't think of anything that wouldn't sound suspicious and anyway, I can't tell even the tiniest untruth without my face turning redder, and my eyes looking everywhere except to the front. I've seen it in my mirror. I guess I will just have to try and change the subject. But every school day, Moeder gives me an 'Eleonore bag' which I am not to open, and I see she is wearing a pair of my grown-out-of old shoes, which are really nearly new, and she is not so skinny and I know it must be full of good things and how would I ever thank somebody if they did exactly the same for me?

June 1941

It couldn't be any worse. Hundreds of families squashed together, and I have to take turns to share a bed with either Papi or Mamie whilst one of them sleeps on the fold-up sofa. The awful thing about here is that you can see the other half of the world through the wire, all going about their business and being happy and free. Every Jewish person is being rounded up and sent to this terrible place, and no one knows what will happen next. It's true that we still may go to school, but we have to pass by Nazi soldiers at the main gates to Jodenbuurt, which is where we now live and show our school pass on the way back. The soldiers never speak, so one day I get brave and say 'Danke' when he hands back the card, and I stare and watch his eyes as they swivel to the ground, and I remember in 'The Jungle Book' that the boy Mowgli always has power over the wolves because the wolves cannot bear to meet his eyes, and for one moment I feel good.

Freyja doesn't know that I have been asked to the zoo again. A kind neighbour has posted on a letter sent to our old address, even though it took some time to arrive. I am to ask for Director Sunier 'in person' and that makes me feel something like a real human being once more.

His office is at the very top of the building in The Gallery. It is good to see a good strong table again, and curtains and chairs with velvet backs, and a Dutch flag alongside that ugly Nazi one, and a kind lady in the next office who makes me coffee and apple cake.

"You need to feel perfectly safe here, Eleonore, come what may," he tells me. "There's nothing to worry about. Look. I tremble sometimes when we have our Germans here, but I know what my responsibilities are. To them and to the animals and to Artis." He walks around the desk as he speaks, just like the important person he is. "And also to our mutual friends, Mrs Scholte and Freyja. You are in danger, Eleonore, of that I am certain, but don't ever be frightened to speak up, and tell anyone, anyone at all, that you will speak to your friend the Director of the zoo about it." And then. "How is Freyja, by the way?" That takes me by surprise because I really shouldn't tell him that we hardly see each other after he has been so kind, so I show him the shoes she has passed on to me. And then I tell him all about how her handwriting is so good and he compliments me on my learning such good Dutch and it's soon as if we have known each other for ages. I wonder if he had forgotten about my interest in art until he says, "One reason I'm so glad you're here is for our paintings. Of course, we keep much more in the zoo than we can ever show, Eleonore. Much has to be stored...So if you're not expected home yet?" I don't tell him that there is no longer anything at home for me, and I don't know whether I can still keep any of my dreams alive, whether as a lawyer, doctor, zoo scientist or the most famous painter ever, but he moves aside our chairs and goes to a winder on the wall, which he turns, and, like magic, a wooden set of steps unfold from the attic trapdoor. "Up you go," he says, "and be very careful. Your father would never forgive me if this was to be your very last visit."

Upstairs is an enormous space, stacked and hung with pictures and he lets me see the vases and flowers and fruit on canvas, which he knows I like best of all. Many are detailed studies of tulips drawn as if they are real, not as brilliantly coloured as if they were on his big table in a vase, of course, but intricate and dazzling in their various forms. "You need to promise me that I can have the first pick of your work one day," he says, but I only smile, because that's just what grown-ups say to make us feel more confident about ourselves.

Afterwards, he walks me to the exit and as we pass the wolves' enclosure. "If you do talk about the zoo," he says, "always call this place the 'Wolf's Lair'. Because then the Germans will think you're talking about Herr Hitler's headquarters, now that he's declared war on the Russians. That's what he calls it."

Chapter 16

The whole school is gathered together, and surprisingly quiet as if the world is about to end. There are some children who have not arrived yet. "Dearest children," from our always kind and friendly Principal. All the teachers are sitting beside her. "We are here today for a very special occasion. One which you should never forget. And a very sad one, I'm afraid. For today, we will say goodbye to some of your friends and our friends, who are no longer allowed to be here, for enjoying fun, for learning, for laughter…" And I notice that Eleonore, my very best friend forever and ever, isn't here.

Back in the classroom, I write over and over, pen pressing through paper.

Why Eleonore?

Why the Jews?

Why now?

Why the Germans?

Why the hate?

Until there is no more space for my suffering, and the writing becomes angrier and angrier and I will not write "Why Freyja?" because, though our parting is cruel and callous, our meeting was a true gift from the Gods of Love.

Chapter 17

I had learned that the Jewish way to say goodbye is to take a small stone and place it on the grave. The stone lasts for eternity. Uncle Paul and I take the tram to Eleonore's old apartment building, and climb the stairs and very gently and with reverence, place the stone by the doorframe where the Mezuzah is no longer fixed. On the 27th of March 1943, I read that there is an attack on the Municipal Register building in Artis in Amsterdam containing the details of seventy thousand Jews. The fire brigade deliberately delays attending the explosions.

Part 2

Chapter 18

Beginnings

For my dearest great-grandchildren. Luc, Irene, Jacqueline, Hannah and Tom.

Here is Grandma's promise at last; to write to you all about my trip to Holland. I had a really wonderful time, but it must be hard for you to imagine me as a little Dutch girl of many years ago.

It's not your country after all. And I was never like those pictures of girls in frilly patterned dresses, with plaits and wearing clogs. In any case, what happened to me can be nowhere near as exciting as you making your own lives. And, as you've only had the 'bits and bobs' from me so far, this is my try at helping you with the bigger picture. Oops! I really must remember! Long ago the thing I was most puzzled about was grown-up sayings, so, if you can, you bigger ones might need to play detective to explain some things to the little ones.

You know about my best-ever school friend, of course. My story didn't end with Eleonore's disappearance. But it was the end of our story together. For a long time, I wouldn't give up hope. Every day I would take a slightly different route to school, and though we had never given each other photographs, I knew one memory in particular; her beautiful and striking eyes would always give her away. I imagined they would act as magnets, drawing me irresistibly towards her, and I often dreamed of her, though sometimes the dreams turned dark and bad and I had to force myself awake. I never made another friend like her after that, and even Dirk and I became distant. It was as if I somehow blamed him for her disappearance because he was an alpha male, and what did he do to help?

At first, I was angry and hateful, for what did anybody truly care? Vader and Moeder, or Uncle Paul or Aunt Myrese? Couldn't they have searched harder, or placed notices on the walls or in papers or something? Nor did I ever speak of this to my own children later on. But it was your parents who persuaded me that, though I had to hold on to hope, we must think only of the dreadful things Eleonore didn't have to suffer; no keeping of pets or favourite journeys, no visits from friends, no cinemas, and always having to put on that hated yellow star wherever you went, and your family and neighbours barred from their jobs, their favourite foods, their normal shopping hours, and people shouting and spitting at you on the streets and…And you will know, I can't easily hold back the tears even now and soon I was sobbing and, though my relatives were very tender towards me, it didn't change a single thing.

We left Holland at the end of November 1945. I say 'we' because by now we were three. Grandpa and me and a little person inside my tummy. Grandpa was my hero in uniform; the Canadians had come to Amsterdam to save us from the Nazis and from starvation and I had fallen in love for a second time; that same yearning for someone you wanted to be with every single moment of the day and night, the images of them carried around in your head that just wouldn't go away, the soft touch and smell of face and skin and fingers. And the shutting out of everyone and everything that wasn't us. And also, still inside, my simmering hatred for Holland, which hadn't tried to save my friend, nor many more, and also for my family, who hadn't understood, or even stood by me when I needed them most. So I vowed I would never return.

Nor did I visit Artis again. How could I walk past that evil sign 'Forbidden to Jews', because I knew it would bring back everything and I had decided to try really hard to forget?

Chapter 19

Middle

I'm on the plane flying to Amsterdam, which has the best airport in the world. There is an underground train station and escalators that take you everywhere so you don't have to walk, lots of colourful illuminated signs which flash on and off, first fast and then slow, and it's just like being in a sci-fi movie. My aunt Myrese doesn't live here anymore, so I take another train, which you reach down the moving stairs, to a city called Zutphen, in the east of Holland, and near where Eleonore must have caught her very first glimpse of her new country. I guess you were so bored of my endless stories of Eleonore, and you will also want to know why I am in the country I swore I would never return to. So I will help. Remember. There are many things that are hidden from us, children.

Myrese's house is large and built in 'the colonial-style', with ornate multi-coloured brickwork and columns and curves of orange beams and you would think you were in the pictures of 'Ali Baba and the Forty Thieves'. We embrace as if we have been friends for years and it is more than painful because our only link since has been the odd 'Happy Christmas' card, unsigned and stamped with a new address.

"Come and meet Erik," she says and we walk together down the tall ornate passageway, with its accompanying wafts of fresh coffee, and our echoing shoes I am back to the sounds of childhood. Unless Mama had asked me to leave them at the door!

Erik is not Paul, which is immediately obvious. Not just in the matter of size – he is nowhere near as tall – but in manner. He is gracious and a little bit shy, not loud and bustling, but immediately wants to know how was my journey and would I like coffee and cake and, "It's so good to have you back in Holland," as if this might be my second home. What does a Canadian bring to friends and family abroad as a gift? (The clue is in our flag) so it has to be the largest single bottle I can fit into my luggage and, of course, you know you cannot visit a Dutch house without a present. But Aunt Myrese, a little tearful now, says I am her best gift ever and what is unspoken between us are the questions and answers the war cut short, and so I will try to be Sherlock Holmes once more and get to the bottom of things.

Erik and Myrese want to learn all about Canada, the life of which they do not know and may not understand, and which is your life too. So that first evening passes pleasantly enough.

Chapter 20

You would have loved it the next day, September 17. It is the day of the fiftieth anniversary of a famous battle between the Nazis and the Allies fighting over a bridge at Arnhem, which is a short distance from Myrese and Erik's. If you haven't already, ask your parents to show you the movie 'A Bridge Too Far', which is famous around the world, except the bridge in the film is not the bridge we see today. Erik tells me it was filmed elsewhere, but no matter. Many brave people were killed that day, including the Germans who defended it, but now I am here, and there are hundreds of parachutes fluttering down from the sky, soldiers in many-varied uniforms, and tanks and military vehicles and brass and pipe bands and so, in a moment, I am transported back to those childhood days and wonder whether Dirk could tell me who is who. You can't imagine how many people are here, and there are lots of speeches I don't understand because I have forgotten almost all my Dutch, but I know that the red berets, the gold braid, the mayoral chains and rows of medals, the singing of the national anthem, the crowd so large that I wonder if the bridge will collapse into the water; all of it means the Dutch are very proud, even though that battle was lost. And I watch as little boys and girls like you, black and brown and white and ebony and some of whose parents weren't born here, link arms and hold flowers together and I remember this little Dutch girl fifty years ago today, whose dreams were shattered again on this terrible day. After that, we all starved for a long time.

I am writing this before sleep and I rather think it would have helped had I filled in more of the background for you. You know lots about lovely Grandpa Jack, of course, even if you never did meet him: the photographs, the medals and his uniform, the 'Holland pictures', the walking stick and wheelchair as he became increasingly frail, and so it's sad, Luc and Irene, that only you of my grandchildren saw him and then as an invalid. You probably imagine that I worshipped him, so often is he mentioned, but it is better if you know that life cannot always be a bed of roses, as that movie says, but that at least you must catch the scent when things get difficult. I know he would have loved this day, especially as his old comrades were likely there, and though we joined the noisy celebrations in the bars afterwards and I asked around, I had no luck in finding any of them.

Chapter 21

We have agreed that today will be a 'clear the air' day, which for grown-ups means saying out loud things we have been too scared or embarrassed or cross about. Erik has kindly suggested he do the shopping for the evening meal, and we will have the whole day to ourselves. As it is still glorious outside, we plump up the cushions on the veranda and even though it is not far into the morning, Myrese pours us a glass of wine and puts out the peanuts and nibbles.

"Where do we start, darling Freyja?" which is what she always called me, and had always made me feel very grown-up.

"At the very beginning," I said, and then, "Anywhere at all, silly Aunty."

Silence, for a moment, for we were children once again.

"Then let me tell you about Uncle Paul. Can I tell you a secret?"

I wasn't quite sure what was coming next.

"I knew you were really in love with him."

"Just like you, Myrese."

"Just like me, Freyja. For a long time anyway."

A pause.

"He became very famous in the war. He had no fear, and you would say he was a hero. Your father too, though in quite a different way."

That was a surprise. "My father?"

"There is much you never knew about your father, Freyja. But you went off in such a…"

She bit her lip then and we both knew she had moved the story on too fast and too far, and she wanted above everything for neither of us to be hurt.

"What do you remember him doing in the war, Freyja? Your father."

"I never really knew. Only that he worked in an office. He never talked about it."

"He never talked about it because it was a very important office. He worked for the Government so that he had to do everything he was told. He had to carry out their instructions. To the letter."

"Did he, Myrese? Many didn't, you know."

It felt an eternity going by until…

"We talked about it many times, your father and mother, and Paul and I. What we could do. And how we could help."

"But you were angry and falling out, I used to hear you."

"Paul and I had a scary time; how to carry illegal newspapers and posters, who needed a radio, how to find hiding places for the undergrounds…"

Hiding places! I had almost forgotten. How could I? Even after all these years. The zoo.

"And Paul, who had studied acting and art, was an expert forger and impersonator. We couldn't let you in on that secret. Nor many others. And not for a single moment was it ever easy."

I was the one struggling with the why question now.

"So how do you forge an illegal passport, Freyja? Do you have any idea?"

I guessed she wasn't waiting for an answer.

"For forging a passport, you need identities, pens, paper, inks and official stamps. And your father had access to all of these."

I didn't know quite what to say. After all, I reasoned, I was only a child.

"And the punishment meted out by the Nazis for 'larceny of official contraband and aiding an enemy?' That was the official term."

"I didn't know those things Myrese. He didn't even try to tell us. Not once."

"There is no way you, nor anyone else, could know, Freyja, even if they were close to you. Those times you just couldn't imagine. It was as if you were enclosed in a glass box and any single movement, even the slightest, it would shatter, and there you'd be, visible and exposed."

"And what did happen? In the end?"

"Many of the stories haven't been told. Still haven't. But it didn't end. For you, after Canada, there was always tomorrow. And I have Erik now. He's a good man. But you should know that afterwards, things went to Paul's head. It happened to many. He had some fame. He was an actor, after all, and he could carry it off. The beret, the clothes, the cheroots, and he was surrounded by pretty young actresses."

I leaned across the table. "I'm sorry. I'm so sorry Myrese, I was so immersed in myself." and she, topping up the glasses.

"Don't be sorry for me, my darling. Life moves on, after all," and at that moment I could see her strength and courage, hers and Paul's, young, and alive, and personable, daring and yet always in danger.

Chapter 22

It's time for me now. "You know something, Myrese? I swore all those years ago that I would never forgive you. Nor my parents."

Her silence gives me the courage to go on.

"After I lost Eleonore, I lost all hope. Life around was all grey, but inside was greyer still. I suppose you would call it depression these days. And I suppose it only went away when I met Jack."

"We liked Jack, you know that, Freyja."

"I didn't see it like that at the time."

"In the same way it seemed you didn't much like your parents either, Freyja."

The words stung. I thought I had put it all behind me by my forgetting.

"You hardly spoke to your father. Your mother was so worried that she asked Paul to help. You met a soldier, twenty years older than you, who swept off your feet. You were carried away with the excitement. Why wouldn't you be?"

"You had no right to interfere, Myrese. That's what I thought."

"You sometimes didn't return home. And where were you? What were they to think? They were worried to death with all that was going on."

I am quiet, because with life comes more understanding, but no less uncertainty.

"Tell me darling Freyja. What would you have done if you were us? Whatever you thought, we were always trying to help. To give the advice your father and mother would have done."

I didn't know what to say. I had loved Myrese. But I was so much overwhelmed by anger.

"Your father was not a forgiving man, I know that, of course. But when it was obvious, you were pregnant…"

"And that was a reason for cutting me out of your lives?"

It just spilt out, and I heard myself, the young girl, again, swayed by emotion and hurt.

I stood and reached over to hold Myrese.

"Please forgive me, Myrese. I should never have said that. I left Holland from spite and hatred. It all happened so very long ago and we have both learned many lessons along the way. The anger you can forgive, but spite never. But there was so much hurt. I loved my parents dearly."

"I know, Freyja. I know. How could you not? But when Paul left, and your mother had lost you, she was never going to let go of her brother. Ever again. And for a time, he became her new life. And then, because we separated on such bad terms, it was me she blamed for everything, as any sister might."

We remained like that, close together, for a very long time, gazing out at that flat green landscape where the sun often only squeezes just above the horizon, and a heron in flight moves across our eye line and the grey clouds whisk on by as if they too are in turmoil.

"You know. I was sometimes ashamed," Myrese said. "You had worshipped Paul, and I knew your heartache if you discovered he wasn't the saint you thought he was, and that he had hurt me every time he didn't come home. I didn't want you and Jack to know that, ever. So he never had your address."

In one way, we had made our peace. From now on, I knew we would try and share our lives, she and Erik, and me and you and who knows, one day you might even wish to visit this place where our lives first began.

That evening we sat around the giant black stove with the chimney that went up through the roof and ate apple cake and slagroom, the Dutch word for cream that I learned soon after oliebollen. I brought out the album I had wanted to share but didn't know if I could, and Erik and Myrese brought out theirs and we learned much more about each other and I asked whether they had ever had planned to have a family and my beautiful Aunt Myrese embraced me and said, "The Germans made sure I never could," before quietly making her way upstairs. And after being kissed goodnight by Erik, I sat silently for hours. In a long marriage, I had never even received a slap, let alone endured a beating.

Chapter 23

I drove west in the rented car quite early in the morning. It was turning from dark to half-light and I had Dirk with me. Not really of course, but in my head. I had carried out my promise to myself, after I had left Holland, to study 'arguments' at university, and to discover more about philosophers. I can tell you all about Spinoza now if you were to ask, but also how difficult it was to study, what with a small child and the expense. Whenever I go into a bookshop, though, I still check the section on animals and particularly wolves, to see if Dirk's name is printed there on the cover, or on the flyleaf. Today, sitting by my side, he is as quiet and shy as ever.

The landscape becomes heavy with trees, and the earth sandy, and we are headed for a place I have never visited before. Just before our horrible war, a museum was opened in Holland to show the largest collection of Van Gogh paintings in the world. The man who paid for it was involved in a bit of a money scandal, but that doesn't mean that this shouldn't be the best ever place to see his paintings. After all, it was his wife who had the courage to search for and choose them.

From the parking areas you can see sculptures; see this one, like a giant child's jack in a game of fives, another is a floating white swan, and then, an elongated spider's web and a giant shiny ball for boules. I take Dirk's hand, and we walk, he and I and, once more, the cool dampness of his skin and how he would turn and twist his fingers as if he wanted to reach to the very centre of me. And this is how you too must enjoy each moment, my children, as if here's the one and only life, and then these moments must always live with you. When your parents were small, before I tucked them in at night and before their goodnight kiss, I always asked, "What has been the very best part of the day?" And whatever their answers, I always loved them, even when they were too tired and only said, "Everything."

We gazed together in wonder at the maestro's paintings. The rich lady, who had first chosen them, said she loved them most for their spirit, and I remembered the artist had once been a preacher in a draughty chapel in England, far from home, and how he must have hoped beyond hope that his words would breathe life and hope into those poor people's lives, and I imagined how disappointed he must have been that he failed to inspire them. He thought he was the world's worst, but you see, he always kept on trying at life. And because there is so much to see, you know that he must have been driven to paint, paint, paint, and so we take a seat, Dirk and I, before a simple still life of 'Flowers in a Blue Vase', and I imagine another absent friend, who was always searching for a simple watercolour to copy, and I reach into my bag and take out the crumpled envelope that I had kept all these years as a memento, and I carefully press out the creases of a sunflower that has been signed 'Drawn by Freya Scholte' but not drawn by me.

It's a long drive to Amsterdam and I have lots of thinking time. I had hidden away my Eleonore for all these years, but Van Gogh's pictures in the Museum have reminded me that there is never a complete escaping from our past.

We are back once more in the high-ceilinged classroom in the Montessori School with its flooding of light from the wide windows, but no light in the soul on this day.

"Dear children. We are here today to mark a very special occasion. One which you should never forget. And a very sad day at that. Today we say goodbye to many of your friends, and our friends too, who are no longer allowed to be here, for enjoying learning, for fun, for laughter..."

I am still searching the room. Where is she? Why is she late?

Of course, I can't remember all the details of what was said that day, but our Principal told us a story so simple and yet so important that it might be included in every book ever written for children like you. And now I try my very best to tell it to you.

"In the very beginning, God created us all as equals. But after the beginning, people began to change. Little by little. If they lived in warm climates, there was little need for heavy clothing, if, by the sea, fish is preferred to meat. Forest dwellers are different from those in deserts and so on. Some have given a name to these groups and called them clans."

"Imagine. You may spend the whole of your life in a clan and that is alright, or you may be curious and wish to move away. Then, most likely, you will meet with other clans and see just how similar or different you are. You may even have a different language and customs, so you will need to learn new things fast. But, over time, you and they will meet and perhaps change each other. On the other hand, some in a clan may grow jealous of other clans and may wish to steal from or hurt them, or they might argue between themselves. They might envy them for their skills or the abundance of crops or cattle. And others may need to move just because of famine or disease. You can see just how complicated everything about life can become."

In my head, I'm still looking for Eleonore. She's not at my side, I can see that. Perhaps she's late and is squeezed in by the door? Perhaps she's ill? Perhaps I'm in a bad dream which is becoming a nightmare?

"For many years, people managed their affairs by 'trading', swapping one thing for another, or working for or helping each other. But over time they invented a currency-money – which had a certain value because it could be kept until needed or lent or borrowed. In all the clans, some people became experts at this, just like the best fisherman or the best sellers of spices, or singers and dancers. And clans invented their own religions too, with their own gods and their speakers of wisdom, called prophets. And the religions were very clear about almost everything, about money, about enjoyment and wrongdoing and even the future."

"As you can imagine, there were many arguments over money and arguments over possessions and between different religions, even between those of us we love. We grown-ups make it easy by calling it 'human nature'. But it can also make people angry and hateful and even want to destroy others, especially if you say some are rich because they charge too much for money, or that they steal other people's husbands and wives, or even that they have killed your God. And it is easier still if the clans have names like 'The Jews' or 'The Gypsies' or 'The Christians' because then you can forget that God, in the beginning, created us all nameless, and you can make them your enemies."

But we should always remember that being equal is not being 'the same' because each one of you has their own special talents. And our own special ways of loving and living.

So, dear children. Promise me. Next time you hear, "That's a Jew," or say, "There's a Gypsy," or believe, "Here's a Communist," think instead, "There's a Rembrandt, the special painter, here's a Spinoza, the deep thinker, there's an Einstein, the clever scientist. All of those things we have tried to teach you. For each of these, it was more important what they achieved, not what was their clan. And because, in the beginning, we were all given our minds and our memories, then for you, and all of your friends who are not here today, you must keep them safe in your heart, and then they will never be lost to you."

Chapter 24

Endings

I never saw Eleonore again. But I know that there are still important things to do before I finally leave Amsterdam. Of course, a visit to Artis, the zoo, and perhaps to find out a little bit more about my father's 'war'. Not many children get to meet their great grandparents, but you will learn many things about them sooner or later. And I don't want it to be something that makes you feel ill of them.

The city has changed a great deal, even though it wasn't bombed or destroyed, and there are many wonderful new buildings alongside the old ones. Some look just like giant children's toy houses with little but glass and windows, and see, there's a house floating as if it's ready for bath time, and here's an entirely black building (that's where the windows came from?) and many more seemingly built from Lego sets. The Dutch are as well known for their modern buildings as for their old windmills. The trams are shinier and sleeker than ever before, but they still rattle and scream over their busy rails. And so many people too! And I should mention money. Holland has notes which look just like Monopoly money and coins that add up to one hundred cents but no guilders or dollars to be seen.

I remember exactly where I need to go to find Eleonore's apartment, and I decide to walk a little. I glimpse the grand Heineken building. I never did learn if the beer was given free in the great strike of 1941, but I know if Paul were here, he would say the beer makers were nasty colonialists anyway. Where else did their sugar come from? I smell oliebollen once more and, children, just guess whether I really do stop and nibble at the sugary treats? I try on some boots to bring home, and I check for directions twice. Just to be certain, mind you. My memory is still in good order, but then you are going to have to keep a check on me as you grow older. For what is a human being without memory?

I catch so many accents and languages that, if I didn't know before, I see that almost every clan in the world has moved around from the beginning of time, and I make a prayer that none of them is too troubled. I feel once more for the stone in my pocket. To be reassured that it's still there. And now I'm nearby and begin to recall the neighbourhood and I expect to see an apartment block. But I don't. Where once were stacked up tall apartments, and maybe doors with their Mezuzahs, there is now a swath of open land, with only bulldozers and pile drivers, and lorries, and soil and cranes populating the landscape. The continually moving figures of workmen in motion remind me of Lowry's painting of tiny people from long ago, and there is constant noise, of the whirring of motors and generators, of drills and saws and thumps and squeaks of wood and metal. And all around the perimeter is a wire fence which first chills me to the bone, but when I ask a workman to explain the shiny texted boards with the drawings and photographs posted there, I understand that here is to be built a place to invite the whole world in, and never again to keep the people out. The foundation stone is already laid, and one day it will be named 'The House of One', where non-believers, and, yes, Christians, and Jews and Muslims will all be welcome to meet or visit for religious holidays, commemorations and celebrations, all the better to learn to understand and live together. It will be for believers in a shared universe, in a sacred building, and though I never did find Eleonore, I know that, along with her stone, her spirit and her soul will always reside here.

Chapter 25

I am as excited today as I was all those years ago. Artis has changed so much, naturally, since the times of war. The direction signs are fresh and colourful, and as full of design tricks as are the modern Dutch buildings. And there are new things such as the Microbe Museum and Planetarium, which I know Dirk and the little ones would love. But more importantly, the idea of this place has become different. It is much more like your classrooms where you see and learn and touch whenever possible. There is more space now for the animals – more even than for the visitors – so that the animals themselves are the rulers, and this is a place where you learn to love them as equal partners on earth and not because they have those children's names you give to your pets at home. You will probably get into arguments as you grow up about whether animals should be kept in 'captivity', but I will leave you to sort that one out for yourselves. I don't think even the great Spinoza has the answer to that one.

I will let you into a secret. I smiled to myself as I paid at the entrance because I wondered what would have happened had I asked to use my free pass from the days of the war, even though I had long forgotten it. And if I had asked for Director Sunier?

But what you will soon learn is that the past seemingly disappears so quickly that it seems as if it is forever lost and, with it, all that matters. But still, it's yours, the past it's your secret. And holding onto the past really matters when it's a question of clans trying to destroy each other.

The bark of the sea lion and the shriek of the hyenas, the squealing of monkeys, the roars of the elephants are direction guides; you don't always need the map they give you and anyway, maps I have found are always difficult to follow. Except for ours, Eleonore's and mine, of course, which is much more than a record of routes and their directions.

"I'm getting more used to my captivity now, though it's a little cramped and very smelly. Even if you love animals, as I do, there's no escaping the stink and the flies. My 'cell' is truly a cell. They have bolted an iron-barred door to the rear of the wolves' enclosure, with just enough room for a fold-up bed, a table and a few books and paper. The paper I need for the plans I draw for making fuses for explosives to fight the Nazis. The funny thing is that I am safe from the animals here because it's me who is locked in! During the day I can merge with the crowds, and after Gert feeds them their meat, I can walk back across the old wooden doors laid across the viewing moat that leads to my prison. Underneath the doors are strong handles that you can hang on to if the Germans arrive unannounced. You do get very wet, of course. The main thing during the day is to try and exercise because you can get very cramped. At night I bend, move away from the bed and do press-ups and stretches, and so I feel healthier than before. Sometimes, too, a rare walk. The animals mean we have sure supplies of fruit and nuts as well as mashed vegetables. I leave the meat for the wolves!

I think I am getting into the mind of zoo animals because I have to fight really hard not to look at the people out there. One early morning I run out of books and paper, I turn and bend, I kneel and jump – just quietly – and now and then I just can't resist, and I'm in a sort of iron grip, and I know I just have to, and I put my face to the gap in the rock and there! Just there. A little girl with the most beautiful blue eyes I have ever seen, like deep inky pools, and I am drawn to them as if to a magnet and I look and look and then she takes her binoculars and lifts them to her eyes and…"

Chapter 26

I remembered that we called this place, 'The Wolf's Lair', because Eleonore was afraid that someone would overhear us as we talked about the zoo, and 'The Wolf's Lair' is where the German leader Adolf Hitler stayed when fighting the Russians, which is one of the reasons, children, that he didn't win the war. He was far too greedy for clan territory. And for a moment or two, I am once more alongside this little blue-eyed princess who always had that funny way of speaking Dutch and who had a good heart and was the wisest person around me then, even when she tricked me by pretending to reveal our secret.

Of course, no-one knew our secret, and I wondered how hard that had been for Eleonore, who knew the zoo far better than me. She had even been the private guest of the Director and had been to see his collection of pictures in the gallery.

We move on. "Now to see something that isn't anything at all to do with our animals," except of course it was similar in some ways, for what was inside was locked up, and very dangerous for the Germans if 'it' got out. We had reached the building where the index cards of the Jews were kept during the war, and I heard once more the story I discovered after I had left Amsterdam. Of the brave women and men who had risked their lives, and how they managed with explosives to destroy many of those names and details, except how tightly were the cards packed together that some did not burn quite through and little did they know, that duplicates were stored elsewhere. And I imagined a Fire Chief who couldn't quite hear the urgent message from the Germans, and him saying, "there's lots of interference on the line," and "could you repeat?" over and over until he might have put his own life in danger. "Of course" – our guide here – "naturally we had lots of help from the people with their local knowledge; of where the lighting and power store was located, or the railings were bent and broken for the 'intruders' to enter, and where the moat was at its shallowest, for then the hoses would go limp and useless some of the time." And I wasn't so much listening and hearing anymore, because I am back again in that day where we two loving girls sat on a bench, with pens and colouring pencils, making a map, and she won't tell me what it is all about, and I am angry and impatient, and I don't trust the wisest friend in the world, and now I silently ask her to forgive me.

And he tells about the man in the wolf's lair, who is an expert in explosive fuses, and I ask in all innocence, "what did they use for timers?" because I knew you wouldn't want all the explosives to go off at the same time.

The man in the brightly-coloured coat and twinkly eyes answered, "why, watches of course. We had a large collection of watches," and I remember that day we spent in the flower market when I saw Eleonore's father with his case of samples, and then they weren't there, and I forgive Eleonore for a second time; this time for not keeping our secret.

Chapter 27

Stay with me, children, for we are on the last lap. Looking back on my writing, I can see I have been a bit 'preachy' but if an old lady cannot pass on her life lessons, who can? And believe me, everyone always has a great deal to learn.

If you ever need to get into a government building and see their records, you will need; Name and Address; Date of Birth; Nationality and Passport or other I.D; Reason for Request; Evidence of connection to the subject of file; Period of Review; Exact dates of Review, etc. etc. So many different ways to make it difficult that you really believe that they don't want you there at all. But I am on a 'why' mission once more, alongside Eleonore, who though not here, has the very same question to answer.

Hard though it is to remember the details, and because Aunt Myrese has helped, I begin to look at the records from my father's old department from the month of April 1941. I think those were the last days when things were normal, and life was not yet grey. I remembered that he told us that he worked for the government on very important papers and had wondered what on earth they might be. Uncle Paul once told me that "The Nazis are more than a little bit stupid. They love paper so much that when this is all over, they will need to build the biggest fire on earth to cover up all their crimes." And then I remembered the fire at the zoo, and the map and the watches and Aunt Myrese's beatings and worried whether it was all one big coincidence, and can you know anything for absolute certainty anyway?

It's a hard slog. The writing is tiny and faded and I need help because my Dutch is not good anymore and some is written in German. I have to tell you that although the officials make it so difficult to begin your search, they are more than helpful after that. But I do have clues because I come across my father's neat signature from time to time and decide to concentrate on that. He was very proud of his writing, which is important in office work, and perhaps why he was always so disappointed in my scribblings. Above his signature are lists of names, some short, some long. But there's sometimes differences between the lists of names. Sometimes they are ringed in red ink. So, I ask for copies of those, and spread them across my workstation and ask myself once more what I would give to have the Sherlock Holmes alongside me, here and now. At first lots of confusion, but then I see it! The pattern. Each of these specially marked lists, whether longer or not, has at least ten names in it. I need the helpful curator once more.

"The officials in this particular department were tasked with connecting details of residents' names with other information on them as if they were making up a giant spider's web. At that particular time, the most important thing for the Germans was to discover where in a particular area of the city most Jews lived. The Germans, of course, thought of these Jews as a disease that must be prevented from spreading before it infected everyone around."

"And what then?" It simply slipped out. Before even a minute's thought, even though the answer must be obvious.

"And then the disease must be moved away."

My journey has become more personal now and my return to the lists of names is sometimes blurred by tears. It is time-consuming, and every notation represents a tragedy. The marked lists all appear similar in having the same pattern until I come upon one signal difference. Against one particular cruel red ring drawn around the names in one of the lists, is a double exclamation mark, heavily accented. And I dread to look again at it because I know now what I will find, and under the 'G' entries – only one Grossman family, a man, his wife and Eleonore the child – the awful reality that must have hit dear Papa that day, that his daughters darling best ever friend and her family were probably doomed. And I cried once more; this time for my father.

Chapter 28

He could see what was happening, my dear Father. And I want you to know, my children, is that we parents want most of all, after loving you, to protect you from harm. And sometimes that means even from disappointment.

At that time, where ten or more Jewish families were living close by each other in this city, they were to be boxed up like furniture and sent to the wire and then most likely, to the camps. And if Father had not stayed silent, and broken my heart, he would not only have put our own lives in danger but the Jews themselves, if they were to begin disappearing in numbers. For where could they go, pursued at every turn by the Nazis? And certain death to their shelterers.

And in that seemingly cruel advice, to spend less time with Eleonore, those words that would separate me from Eleonore, the love of my young life, he was protecting me, and sheltering me from a hurt he knew would surely come. For few places at that time were safe, except that, for some, for a short time, in a large city. In a special place in Amsterdam, where the animals too, were treated with the same respect as the humans. And because of the goodness of the human heart.

I imagined myself again on that last day of mine and Eleonore's life together, when in my rage, I scratched my questions right through the paper. I can see the list right now. Right there before me. And, in my imagination, I take out my pen.

Why Eleonore?
Why the Jews?
Why now?
Why the Germans?
Why the hate?

And carefully, but now, much more hopefully, add to the list

Why Artis?

It is for you, dear children, to complete the story. I have spent a whole lifetime questioning. Now your lives must be added to my lives, must be added to others' lives right up until the end of time. But always remember that one most important thing – my father's advice. To forever keep asking the 'why' question. Over and over again. For, if you really try, and you get even just some of the answers, you will become masters and mistresses of the entire universe, for you will have uncovered its deepest secrets.

Postscript

Some years later, a call went out for stories and recollections from those and their shelterers who 'disappeared' in Holland during the years of occupation by the Germans. These fragments were found amongst them.

(Undated)

I won't give up my diary, whatever happens. And I will write as if nothing has changed between us, even if I can never see F again. Papi has taught us all to be very careful about what we say, who we contact, and where we go, because the Nazis are everywhere, including those who are Dutch and who should be on our side. He says I shouldn't even think of visiting her, or the M. School, because it will put them, as well as us, in grave danger. There are no telephones here either, so the only way to make contact with anyone is to write one's message and have it delivered by hand. There are Dutch strangers who will do this, even without payment, which just shows the goodness in people.

Some of our friends here are more optimistic because the Nazis have recently invaded Russia, which is supposed to be its friend and ally, and Russia is one of the biggest countries in the whole world, so that gives us a chance, except that must mean that things will go on for an eternity. But because no one here is allowed to work at their jobs, we can only work for each other, so then there is the problem of where does the money come from? There are ways, but I am not allowed to tell, and this is one of the worst things, that we have to have secrets about everything as if we are the guilty party; about where we get our food and supplies, who we know and who we meet, what we own and what we read, and even where we pray, though who can believe in anything anymore? But we mustn't lose heart, for the great Sherlock Holmes himself got 'down in the dumps' sometimes. Admittedly, he had his violin to cheer him up. And in 'The Adventures of Sherlock Holmes' there is a story called 'The Red-headed League' where the rogues build a tunnel to steal the money so that even if the

Nazis build a wall around us to replace the fence, we can always dig ourselves out. I only wish I had my F here to help me sort things out.

(Undated)

For my dearest F. I just know you will want to find out what is going on. So where do I start? I miss you terribly, of course, but you will be pleased to learn that I am still a 'little teacher' because the younger ones here need help to keep learning and understanding things for the future. The main thing is for them to forget all the terrible things that go on around them, even if for only a few hours, so we play lots of 'let's imagine' games. They can be dragons breathing fire, or princesses in their finery (we're fast running out – HINT!) or ghosts which they like a lot because they can see through people and they come back when you die. And do you remember how we learned to cook at the M.S. when you only had scarce or unusual ingredients? That comes in handy. Don't imagine that we starve, but it is harder and harder to get hold of things. I also took a few of the toddlers to 'our favourite place' because I still have my pass, and if I ask for G at the gate, he will always come and collect us. The wolves are still there (code). Before we visit, I teach the little ones 'imaginary' Christian names as a precaution, which is not so difficult because they all have best friends from a previous time. Also, you might not know this, but there are animals that like sweet things, such as bears which will eat almost anything (hint.)

Papi has a 'new job!' Because he has spent his whole life in watches, he now attempts to mend them when they break.

He has all the tools too, but I haven't a clue where they have come from. Time goes much more slowly here and so people spend more time checking it, which is a paradox, as grown-ups say. I know you will smile at that, for we detectives have spent our whole lives searching out the clues to the grown-ups! Incidentally, there is a professor here who says I shouldn't use so many exclamation marks "as it is a sign of sloppy writing" So!!!!!!! To him.

Now F, you can tell me honestly what is happening between Dirk and you? Existing here with people living on top of each other, I can't help but notice much more about people's ways of loving and sadly, even of hating. And, after all, there is no one here to betray your secrets to anymore.

It's not a boast but, for myself, I am 'spoiled for choice', as they say, but no one has those special qualities that you have, or that you always listened to everything I said, however ridiculous it seemed.

(undated)

You remember all those silly games we played when we were together? Well. Here's one called 'Riddles'.

Who am I?

Are you ready?

I have a furry skin.

No, I am not a wolf. (I guessed you'd say that.)

I eat mainly nuts and fruit.

I sometimes walk on all fours.

I said I wasn't a wolf, silly. I said 'only sometimes'.

Remember, we saw the Tarzan and Jayne film? I can climb.

There's a clue.

Okay, you got it.

Now, where am I?

I can see, but I can't be seen.

I am not allowed out to swing on trees.

But I am safe.

What now?

I have befriended a dog.

It is a St Bernard. It can find people, however hard it is. One day I hope it will get my stories to you. With love. Always.

Historical Background

In spite of their soldiers fighting bravely, Holland was overwhelmed by the Germans on May 10, 1940. The Dutch had been neutral in the wider war thus far, but had inferior weaponry and fighters and poor defences. Their Queen fled to England. From that time on, some Dutch citizens engaged in passive and active resistance and suffered the consequences. Many were forced from their homes, sent to work as forced labourers in Germany, starved, or deported. By the end of the war, three-quarters of the Jewish population of Holland had been deported or killed.

On 22–23 of February 1941, raids on the Jewish quarter led to the arrest of more than four hundred men, and protests broke out across the city, culminating in a General Strike on the following days. Nevertheless, others benefited from the German presence, including some co-operating police and those in the Dutch-Nazi Party, and professionals and civil servants who stepped into the shoes of those denied or sacked from their posts. Some had been angered by the success of Jews, who had been resourceful enough to 'cross the Amstel' to the better side of the city. There were even those who joined the German military and fought on that side.

Those that took up arms against the occupiers engaged in sabotage, delaying or attacking transport links, smuggling, arson, and forgery; others simply 'disappeared' underground. For their bravery, many were shot or imprisoned. For some time in those years, the zoo Artis in Amsterdam was the hiding place for between 250–300 men and women escaping forced labour or death. They included communists, Jews and their families. The zoo's Director really was Mr Sunier, whom the children called Mr Armand, his Christian name, and the sculptor Jaap Kaas worked in hiding there. My story is an attempt to do justice to all those often undocumented heroes, who ensured that not a single one of those hidden was ever discovered or betrayed.

On March 27 1943, fires were set in the Municipal Registry based at the Artis zoo in Amsterdam, where the records of 70,00 Jews were held. Even though the fire brigades were delayed, sadly fewer than 15% of those records were destroyed. The attackers were betrayed and shot.

Although almost all of the south of Holland was freed by the end of 1944, the botched effort to take the bridge at Arnhem meant much of the northern Netherlands, then starved over winter. It wasn't until May 5, 1945, that the whole country of Holland belonged to its people once more.

'The House of One' does exist, but in Berlin. It is currently being built; its foundation stone having been laid in 2020.